A Boy A Bike Alaska!
Mt. Shasta to Denali

Warren Carlson

ISBN 978-1-954896-07-9 Paperback
ISBN 978-1-954896-1-47 Hardbound
ISBN 978-1-954896-08-6 ebook
Library of Congress Control Number: 2022908148
First edition July 2022

Author Disclaimer:
   The highways, parks, and towns Jack visits on his trip are real but this is a work of fiction. Some details concerning campgrounds, restaurants, and roadside attractions are fictionalized. Names, characters, places, and incidents either are the product of the author's imagination or are used fictitiously. Any resemblance to actual persons, living or dead, events or locales is entirely coincidental.

Maps and illustrations by
   Anthony LeBeau, Art by LeBeau, artbylebeau.com

US Map by
   Ad_hominem/Shutterstock.com

Cover images
Denali by Connie Taylor/FathomTwist.com
Highway image by AlxYago/Shutterstock.com
Motorcycle image by EB Adventure Photography/Shutterstock.com

Publisher's Cataloging-in-Publication data
Names: Carlson, Warren H., author.
Title: A boy a bike Alaska! / Warren Carlson.
Description: Anchorage, AK: Fathom Publishing Company, 2022.
Identifiers: LCCN: 2022908148 | ISBN: 978-1-954896-07-9 (paperback) | 978-1-954896-08-6 (ebook)
Subjects: LCSH Motorcycling--Alaska--Fiction. | Alaska--Description and travel--Fiction. | BISAC YOUNG ADULT FICTION / Action & Adventure / General | YOUNG ADULT FICTION / Boys & Men | YOUNG ADULT FICTION / Travel & Transportation / Car & Road Trips
Classification: LCC PS3603.A75335 B68 2022 | DDC 813.6--dc23

fathompublishing.com
Fathom Publishing Company
P.O. Box 200448
Anchorage, Alaska 99520-0448
Telephone / Fax 907-272-3305
Printed in the United States of America

Table of Contents

Dedication

A thank you to my wife, Lucille Nichols and to Connie Taylor at Fathom Publishing for shepherding this book from its rough form to a finished manuscript. And a thanks to the English teachers in my life who encouraged me to work hard and succeed.

I am also grateful for all the opportunities I have had for adventures here in the United States and several foreign countries. I hope young readers of this book will be motivated to have their own adventures.

And finally, I also want to express my gratitude to the kind and friendly people I met on the road during my own motorcycle journey to Alaska. You were the inspiration for this book.

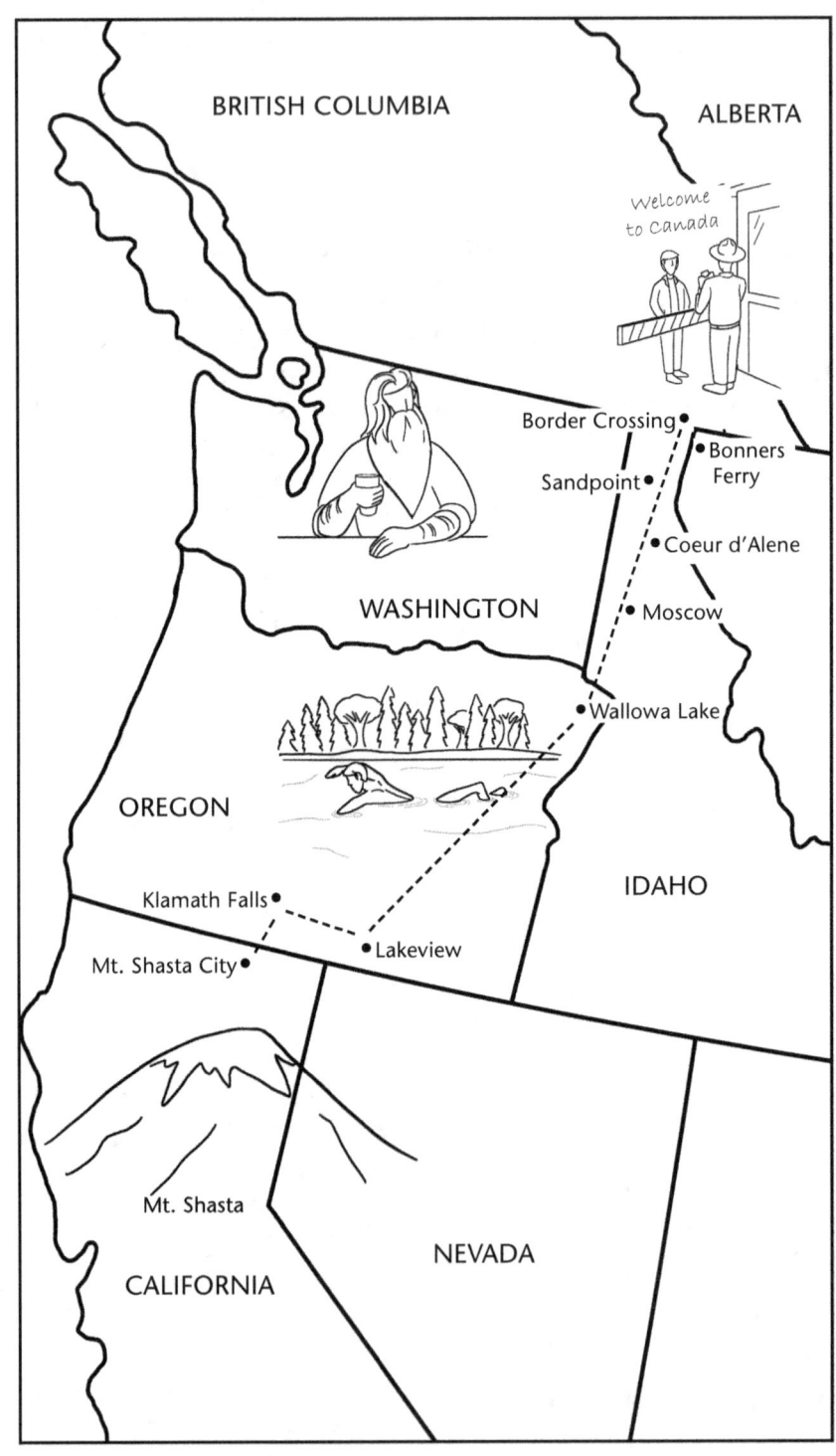

Chapter One

Look Out World

"Don't you dare get a tattoo, Jack Iverson!" my mother, Alice, called to me as I was pulling out of our driveway on my motorcycle, bound for a summer job at my Uncle Pete's fishing lodge in Alaska. It was the day after high school graduation in Mt. Shasta City, California. My ride was an older Honda Shadow I'd rescued from my cousin's barn several months earlier.

With two flat tires, loose wires, a broken headlamp, frozen cylinders, a mouse-eaten seat, and a smashed-in gas tank from the last time it had been ridden, it was a mess! I paid six hundred dollars for it with money I had saved from mowing lawns, shoveling snow, and working for my dad, Richard, on weekend construction projects.

My dad helped me get it home with his big pickup truck. The front tire was frozen in a twisted shape from the accident, so we had to drag the heavy bike up the ramp. We leaned on the side of the truck looking at it. Not talking. Had I made a mistake? I bet we were both thinking how much it would cost in labor and money to make it rideable. "The tires are beyond rescue," Dad said. "I'll buy you a new set, but the rest is up to you."

Five months and another four hundred dollars later, and the help of a local mechanic, I completed the repairs. I took my girlfriend, Allison, on some local rides. She was off to college in the fall while I was uncertain about my future plans. I liked to work and I liked being outside. Twelve years in classrooms was enough. My parents expected me to fly to the job in Alaska, but I decided to ride the bike. Why leave my newfound love behind when we were just getting to know each other? I had mapped out a route that would take me all the way to Denali on mostly two-lane roads and without going through any cities.

There was a scene when I told my parents my plan. Well, there was a scene with my mother. She wasn't worried that I would misbehave, but she was worried about other drivers and my lack of motorcycle experience. She had insisted that I take a safety course taught by a retired motorcycle cop. She was also concerned about me working for Uncle Pete. He was a lifelong bachelor who my mother thought was wild and drank too much, while my father said his brother was smart and knew how to run a business. I was eighteen. I decided.

Saying good-byes was not easy. Allison was leaving for the summer to be a camp counselor. She and I had been close all through high school. My lifelong friend, Davie, who had spent as much time as possible in shop class, had already started work as a welder on a local bridge building project. I knew I would miss my parents, but it was time to leave the nest. I had packed and repacked my camping gear until everything fit on the bike. My mechanic had given the Honda a last inspection and given me a list of daily safety checks and a maintenance schedule. "Take care of the bike and the bike will take care of you."

While the bike idled in the driveway, Allison, who lived next door, hugged me and kissed me for the first time in front of my parents, then fled to her house, crying. My father shook my hand and whispered, "I wish I was going with you." Mom hugged me three times before I managed to get on the bike.

At the end of our block, I made a slight detour so I could drive down Mount Shasta City's main street. Despite my helmet and face shield, I hoped someone would recognize me. When I stopped for a red light, Mrs. Goodyear was sweeping the sidewalk in front of her bookstore.

"Jack? Is that you? Are you going camping in Lassen Park?"

"Nope. North to Alaska."

"That sounds wonderful! Oh, the light changed."

I roared away. I guess to show off. I turned right at the corner and leaned into the curve of the on-ramp to the highway. "Be one with the bike," I said to myself. "Be one with the road." It was hard not to think about all I was leaving behind, especially Allison. Without realizing it, I had slowed down. A semi-truck passed me. The bike wobbled when hit by the wall of turbulent air. I took the bike up to seventy and passed him. I was on my way. I was free! But being on Interstate Five did not feel like an adventure. Either I was passing semis or being blocked in by the large trucks.

As planned, I turned off at Weed, California. Highway 97 out of Weed goes northeast to Klamath Falls, Oregon. Some truckers use this route, but they tend to bunch up, leaving me the room to cruise. I needed to be at my uncle's lodge by June sixteenth which gave me fourteen days to get there. I planned to average three hundred miles a day. My father had ridden across the country when he was young, and he had insisted that I schedule a few rest days for safety reasons.

I slowed down for a last look at Mt. Shasta, my mountain. My goal for the day was a campground north of Burns, Oregon. Three hundred miles. From my day trips I'd learned that the concentration needed to ride a bike safely was greater than when driving a car. I did my best to relax into the trip. Fortunately, at Klamath Falls, Oregon, the truckers stayed on 97 north while I turned east on 140. My well-tuned bike hummed along. I felt proud. I sang into my face shield. My mother sang in the church choir, but I had inherited my father's uncertain voice. It didn't matter. I sang to celebrate.

I climbed from range land to pine forests, then over Quartz Mountain Summit and down to the ranches outside of Lakeview, Oregon, where I stopped for lunch. I did feel a bit lonely. I already felt far from home. I hadn't seen another motorcyclist. I was ready though. Outside of cities, it was a tradition to salute other riders by extending your left arm down and to the side, a gesture I had practiced.

This will sound crazy, but I carried a two-piece fishing pole in plain sight on my luggage, even though I had no intention of fishing. A friend said it would be a conversation starter and he was right. At gas stations, and in parking lots and campgrounds, people would see the pole and say things like, "Where are you headed? Going fishing?" A conversation that usually ended with my new acquaintance saying, "I wish I was headed north." My dream was other people's as well. I didn't mind sharing.

After lunch and topping off the tank (a full tank was good for approximately a hundred miles), I turned north on Route 395 to Burns, Oregon. I skirted Lake Abert, an unusual body of water bordered by alkaline flats and weird rock formations. Sulfur hot springs and an occasional geyser lined the shores.

I reached my first campsite of the trip at eight o'clock. After a dinner of canned beans and Boston brown bread, I climbed into my roomy two-person tent, which was big enough for me and my gear. I blew up my air mattress, slipped into my sleeping bag, folded my Carhartt jacket for a pillow, turned on my headlamp, and started to read *Annapurna* by Maurice Herzog, an account of climbing that 8,000-meter peak in the Himalayas, a parting gift from Allison, until I was sleepy. On that first night and almost every night of the trip, I slept like a logger, heavily, without dreams, while at home I would often lay awake, worrying about something.

I woke at dawn. There was dew on the grass, a mountain chill to the air, and a problem I had not anticipated. Long distance motorcycle riding requires an iron butt. After riding three hundred miles the previous day, I was painfully aware that I did not have one. Just sitting at the picnic table for a breakfast of pancakes, powdered eggs and coffee was painful. My bike had a narrow, flat, street bike seat instead of the curved, padded seats I saw on Honda Electra Glide touring bikes. My goal for the day was to camp at Wallowa Lake, Oregon. I hoped the burning sensation would lessen by the time I stopped at John Day, Oregon, for lunch. It did not.

After lunch, I got gingerly back on the bike. There was absolutely no comfortable way to sit. I wondered if the people having lunch on the patio were watching me squirm. "It's just a problem to solve," I said to myself as I pulled out of the parking lot. A short time later, I stopped at a rest area and tied a folded shirt on the seat. It didn't work. I felt desperate. Either I solved the problem or what? The trip was over? That was unthinkable.

At Ukiah, Oregon, I found a drugstore and bought a hemorrhoid donut. At the far corner of the parking lot, I inflated it, covered it with a shirt, and tied it on the seat, hoping no one would notice. It worked. Every day I filled it with less air until I didn't need it at all. Iron butt by stealth.

There was only the road, the bike, and me. At one point, a group of six motorcyclists caught up with me and invited me to join them. I tagged along, but on the first section of open highway, the whole group accelerated to maybe ninety miles an hour. I chose to take in the scenery at a slower speed. During the day's ride, I let my mind wander. I thought about luck and my best friend, Davie. He lived in a trailer park next to the river with his dad. Last spring there had been a flash flood that hit the trailer park just as Davie was returning from school. While trying to save his father's tools, a surge swept the trailer downstream. Davie jumped out just before it sank. He was washed against the brick wall of an abandoned factory. On the brick wall was a round metal ring. He grabbed it. If the ring hadn't been there ...?

My dad and I heard about the flood and raced to the trailer park. Davie was still hanging onto the ring. He looked terrified. My dad backed his truck into the water, stood on the bed, and threw a rope he had weighted with a piece of wood into the river. It floated to the brick wall almost directly below my best friend. The water was rising fast. To save himself, Davie had to let go of the ring, fall into the water, and grab the rope. I think that was the first time in my life I really prayed. He made it. Dad pulled his truck forward, reeling Davie in like a fish. I waded into the water, helped him stand and hugged him. Luck. If there hadn't been that ring? If we hadn't shown up in time? For graduation, I gave him my mountain bike. He'll be there for me when I get back home in September.

At La Grande, Oregon, I crossed over Interstate 84. One glimpse of that highway crowded with trucks convinced me that state roads were the way to go. I would follow State Highway 82 to Wallowa Lake. When I stopped for gas, a biker on a Harley pulled in. In a friendly manner he said, "Hey Kid, with all that stuff on your bike, I thought I was following a Lazy Boy recliner down the road. How far are you going?"

"Alaska, to work at my uncle's lodge near Denali National Park," I answered proudly. The biker eyed the shirt-covered lump on the seat of my bike but didn't say anything about it.

"This is my second day on the road," I added.

"Bike running okay? Your idle sounded a little rough."

"On hills. It doesn't seem to have the power it did."

"It's the gas. These small stations, your gas probably has water in it. Put in an additive. They'll sell you some. Should take care of it."

"Thanks. Jack," I said, offering my hand.

"Henry. Wish I had the time to go with you. Take care of the bike and ...?"

"The bike will take care of me."

"Right on, Brother. Good luck with the fishing."

I went inside and bought the additive. Before leaving, I stood behind the bike and looked at it. It did look ridiculously overloaded. And it did look sort of like a motorized recliner. I guess I had been making people smile just by driving down the highway. I decided that evening, at the campground, I would unpack everything and see what I could live without.

Henry was right. The bike ran better with the additive. One less thing to worry about. About an hour after leaving the gas station, I caught up with an RV chugging slowly up a hill. There were no passing lanes. When it looked like there was a straightaway where I could pass, I rode just over the center line so I could see around the RV. Finally, there was an opening! I accelerated. Suddenly, a log truck came around the corner at the end of the straightaway. The opening seemed much smaller than it had a moment before. The angled gap between the RV and the truck was disappearing. The RV was not slowing down!

Brake or accelerate? Now or never. I twisted the throttle all the way back. I shot through the gap to the blast of the truck's air horn and the screeching of its brakes. A few miles down the road, I turned into a pull-out with a historic marker. I pretended to read it as the RV drove past. The driver waved. It was not a friendly wave.

While I rode, I thought about my near accident and how one bad decision could totally screw up someone's life. I realized that not only had I been terrified but I had felt very alone. I thought about my life so far—how easy it had been. How lucky. I decided to call my parents once I reached the campground and reassure them the trip was going well. I didn't plan on mentioning the near accident—or the hemorrhoid donut.

I stopped for lunch at a gas station and bought two burritos, a coke, and a small pizza for later. I also bought six postcards with a photo of a "jackalope," a non-existent animal consisting of a rabbit with antelope horns. I sat at a picnic table to write out cheerful messages. I settled onto the partly inflated donut, looked at the map in its plastic sheath strapped to the gas tank and ventured on.

I reached the campground at Wallowa Lake, Oregon, about seven-thirty. It is a beautiful, pristine lake with the mountains of the Eagle Cap Wilderness in the background. After setting up camp, I took the donut off the bike and hid it in the tent, took off my heavy riding boots, changed into my bathing suit and flip-flopped down to the beach. It was deserted. I followed my regular routine of standing in the water up to my knees until my legs no longer felt cold, then falling backwards screaming. I swam a hundred yards from shore and floated on my back. Then I swam underwater for as long as I could just for fun. I love to swim. I had been asked to try out for the high school swim team, but couldn't see the point of swimming back and forth in a chlorinated pool just to prove I was faster than someone else.

Back in camp, I unloaded my panniers to determine what I could do without. At the bottom of one, I was surprised to find a camera and a journal—a camera I had hoped to buy but felt I couldn't afford. There was a note from Mom asking me to take pictures and write in the journal so I could share the trip when I got home. From Dad, there was a hundred dollars in an envelope and a note saying, "Every man needs a little walking-around money."

I decided I needed everything I had packed to be comfortable. The next day I planned to ride all of Idaho, south to north, and cross into Canada.

Chapter Two

Strange Brew

It felt good to be going north instead of northeast. I rode up out of the valley, down to the Grande Ronde River, and out of the canyon on the road locals call "Rattlesnake" for the way it curls back on itself. I rode most of it in second gear, slowing into the curves, finding the right line, and accelerating. It was much like running gates in a ski race. I came out on a high plain. There were few towns or even farms. One town had only thirty-two residents.

I descended to the Snake River and crossed to Lewiston, Idaho. After climbing the steep grade out of the canyon, I cruised past Moscow, Idaho. The wheat fields were green. The stalks waved in the wind. The world was bursting with life. I shared the biker's wave with other motorcyclists.

I rode through the Coeur D'Alene Indian Reservation, careful to obey the speed limit. I was tired but soldiered on to Sandpoint, Idaho. I crossed the two-mile bridge across Lake Pend Oreille and stopped at a Sandpoint city park for a swim. The natives seemed friendly. A small town with a lake and a ski area. If I ever moved away from my hometown, it would be to a town like Sandpoint.

An hour later I hit a wall of fatigue. Even the motorcycle seemed tired. Luck was with me. Just as I needed it, there was a campground. I got the last tent space. I hadn't stopped for groceries so, after setting up the tent, I doubled back to a bar and grill. There were only four trucks and no cars in the parking lot. A waltz was playing on the jukebox. A lone couple was dancing, or maybe just holding each other up. Soon after I ordered, the world's hairiest man came in and sat down at the lunch counter three seats away from me.

I did my best not to stare. I guessed staring would not be a good idea. A dirty blond mane fell over the man's shoulders down to his butt. His beard, which seemed to grow out of his entire face, was so long it appeared to be folded over on his lap like a large, hairy napkin. His mustache jutted over his lips. He had bushy eyebrows that had turned gray.

Four loggers arrived wearing red suspenders, jeans cut off above the boot tops, oily and covered with sawdust. The WHM looked at me as if daring me to say something. My order of burger, fries and a coke arrived. It was surprisingly good.

"That your bike outside?" one of the loggers asked.

"Yes," I answered, relieved that I had removed the donut. "Going to Denali National Park, Alaska."

"Huh, you must think you're tougher than you look. Good luck."

"Thanks."

A woman came in and greeted the loggers with a joke I didn't quite hear. She had a tough-looking body like she might be a truck driver and ride a Harley. She had short, red hair, purple lipstick, and hoop earrings. I hoped she would sit down with the loggers. She didn't. She sat down two seats to my left. She stared at me. I concentrated on my fries. I sensed she was playing some kind of game. I just wanted to eat and go to the campground to sleep. A beer automatically appeared in front of her.

"Does your mommy know you're out after dark?"

"She knows I'm on my way to Alaska," I mumbled.

"Is she worried you might fall in with the wrong crowd?"

"She's worried I might fall off my bike," I said. Then I stupidly added, "Or get run down by a logging truck."

"Hear that, Boys? His momma is worried he might get run down by a logging truck.

"And she won't be there to kiss your owie and make it better."

"Geez, Alice," one of the loggers said. "Give the boy a break. We don't care if he makes it to Alaska or not."

"You're right, why should I give a darn about some pup," Alice said as she drained her beer and joined the loggers. I went back to my meal. I ate as fast as I could. I wanted out of there. At the loggers' table, Alice was telling a story. She laughed while she talked. Another slow song on the jukebox ended. The couple that had been "dancing" went to a booth and fell asleep. I kept eating. The order of fries was huge.

"Give us a song," said the WHM to Alice in a clear, well-modulated voice that from a gnome came as a surprise. Alice turned on the karaoke machine and sang a country western ballad. She sang well. I wondered if she sang in a church choir and wasn't as tough as she appeared to be.

"You're next, Cowboy," the WHM said to me. I panicked.

"I really can't sing," I said, looking around the room for support. The WHM decided to make this personal.

"Anyone can sing a Willie Nelson song. You wouldn't want to disappoint old Willie, would you?" His voice carried to the loggers' table. They stopped talking and looked at me.

"Every new person here has to sing," the WHM declared.

I suddenly realized that I was far from home. I managed to put some steel in my voice when I responded, "I'm not really here. I was just hungry."

The WHM looked at me with contempt then seemed to lose interest. Laughter came from the loggers' table. I wasn't sure if it was at my expense. I finished my meal, left a tip, and stood up slowly. I felt like a sheriff in an old western. I walked to the door unsure if the drinkers were staring at me or not.

As I rode away, I wondered what the WHM could do for a living? For safety reasons, running a chain saw or welding or machine work were clearly out of the question. *Perhaps with his commanding voice, he might have a career as a telemarketer,* I thought.

That night, waiting to fall asleep, I thought about the people at the tavern. I thought about the different ways people lived their lives. I thought about telling Allison about the WHM and pictured her laughing. I slept late. I woke to the sounds of people breaking camp: children calling, cars starting, and doors banging.

It was a beautiful morning for a ride. I was falling in love with my Honda and the open road. I enjoyed smoothly shifting through the gears, rapidly accelerating when necessary, the purr of the well-tuned engine, the hum of the tires on the pavement, leaning into the corners, and learning the subtleties of how some corners were well engineered and some were not. I felt I was doing a good day's work.

It was a beautiful day. There was little traffic, and I was excited about entering Canada, my first foreign country, but I missed Allison. We had been boyfriend-girlfriend all the way through high school in a quiet way. Unlike some of our friends who were couples with a capital "C," we were relaxed together. We didn't always need each other's company. I had an after-school job and Allison was on our championship softball team. We didn't see that much of each other during the spring. Without talking about it, we accepted that our future was unknown. I tried to give the road my complete attention, but the words "your future is unknown" seemed stuck in my head.

As I rode north, I thought about things. I was enjoying my new feeling of being free. I realized I had felt ... crowded ... most of my life. My parents ... we love each other, but they had a lot of rules and expectations. One of my mom's favorite sayings if I asked for something was, "Are your legs broken?" By age ten, I got myself up, made my own lunch, helped my dad cook breakfast, and got to school on time. They demanded that I get all A's and B's in high school. "I earned this trip," I said out loud to myself. "Darn right!" This escape to Alaska was my third outdoor adventure.

In the fall of my sophomore year, my parents were called away when my mother's cousin was injured in a car accident. They were going to be gone overnight. It was a school day. The weather was mild. The idea to hike into the woods east of town and spend the night alone came to me when I was standing on the front porch as they drove away.

After a restless day at school, I hiked into the woods and reached my campsite just before dark. I had a warm sleeping bag, a fire, food, Mt. Shasta lit by starlight, and the stars themselves. I hardly slept. Watching the stars come out, I imagined I could feel the earth turn as the stars moved across the sky. I was not afraid and I wasn't lonely. When I arrived at school the next morning, I felt older than my friends. Davie and Allison were the only ones I told.

When I was seventeen, my mother decided we should climb Mt. Shasta as a family. My mother is a great believer in setting goals and working hard to achieve them. She works in a real estate office as a secretary, but next spring she will graduate from our local community college with a certificate as a legal aide.

It bothered her that Mt. Shasta was in our backyard but she had never seen the view from the top. April first was the start of our training period. After dinner, we would all climb a hill south of town. She had a stopwatch and kept a journal. My father smoked. Not a lot, but enough. The training was hard for him, but he didn't complain. He wanted to be part of the team. Our goal was to make the climb July first. When the big day came, my dad decided to be our support team instead of trying for the summit. We camped at ten thousand feet. He got up before dawn and made us a big breakfast over a camp stove. At first light, my mother and I started the climb that turned out to be the hardest physical thing either of us had ever done. When we stood on the summit together, I almost cried. I guess from pride and relief. My mother did cry. The world below was beautiful and waiting for me.

WELCOME TO CANADA

"Please step off the bike and take off your helmet and sunglasses."

I did as he asked. For a moment, I felt a flash of panic that I wouldn't be let in.

"I.D.?"

I took out my identification from the inner pocket of my jacket. The customs officer stepped into his kiosk and ran my I.D. through a computer check and returned.

"All set except for one thing," he said.

"What is that?" I asked.

"I'm not sure we allow the importation of hemorrhoid donuts into Canada," he said with a straight face and then laughed. I laughed with him, but I didn't mean it.

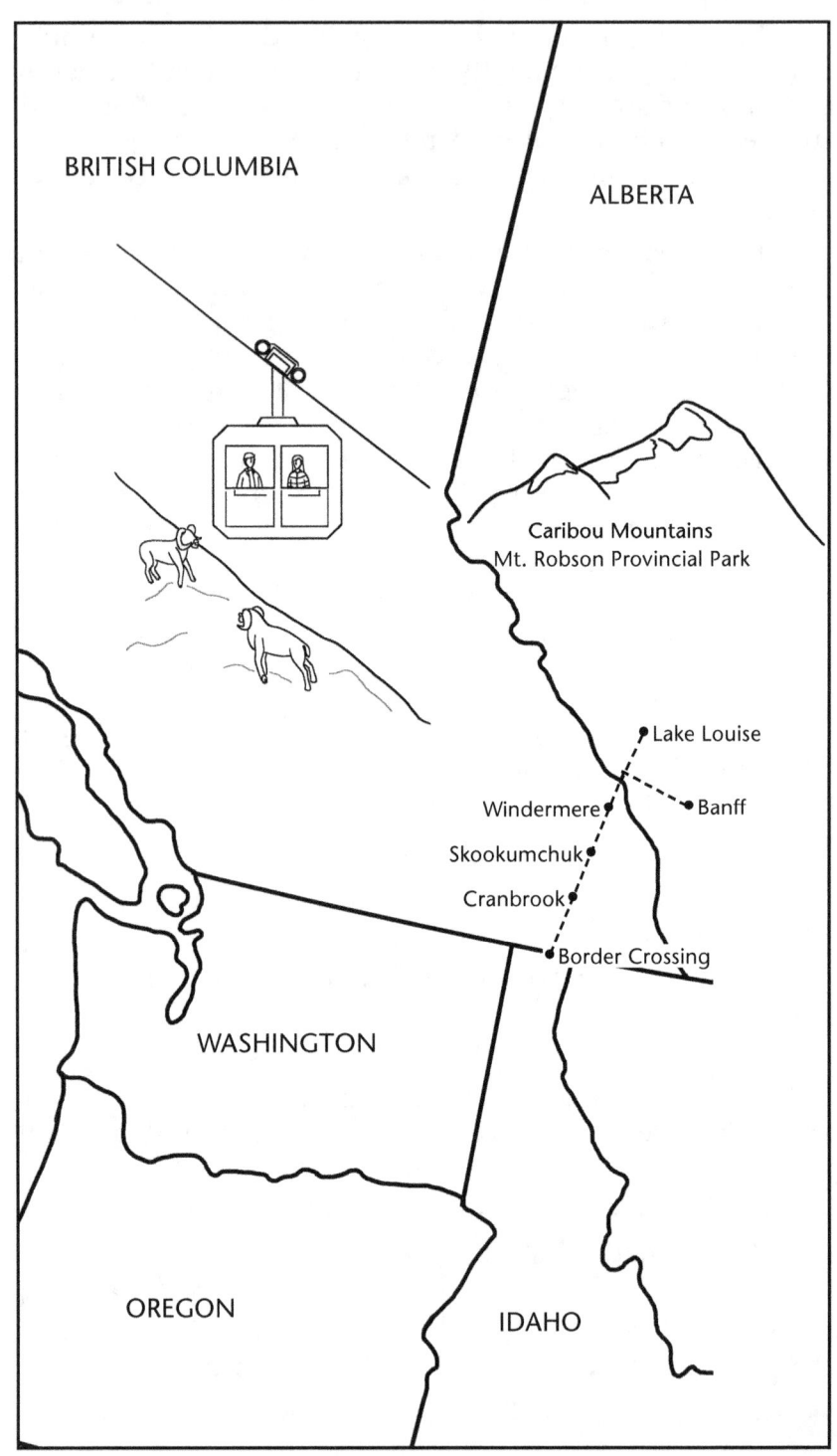

Chapter Three

Good Neighbors

On Route 93-95, I continued north—NORTH! I stopped for a late breakfast at Cranbrook, rode through the town of Skookumchuk, and stopped at Fairmont Hot Springs for a soak. North of Windermere, at the intersection of 93 and 95, I took 93 to Banff National Park and found a spot at a campground near Lake Louise. I decided to give myself a day off. I planned to ride the ski area gondola and spend some time WALKING instead of riding the bike.

After a walk down to the lake to stretch my legs, I was writing in my journal when an RV pulled up to the space next to me. A girl about my age got out and stood next to a tree close to the parking space so the driver could see her in his rear view mirror in case he got out of alignment. He did an excellent job of backing in. I kept glancing over at the girl while they set up camp. I wondered if I should feel guilty. It had only been a few days since I had said good-bye to Allison. Today would be her first day at summer camp. For a while, I pretended to be writing in my journal. The girl caught me looking at her and gave a kind of half wave. I waved back. She walked over to the border between our camps.

"Hi. My parents wondered if you would like to join us for coffee and apple pie?"

"Sure. Can't pass up an invitation like that."

"I'm Angel from Madison, Wisconsin."

"Jack from Mt. Shasta City, California." Angel was tall, athletic looking, and had that relaxed confident look of girls who know they are attractive. I liked her immediately.

"Mom, Dad, this is Jack from Mt. Shasta City, California. Jack, my parents Ariel and George."

Our conversation was interrupted by the attempt of the driver of a pick-up pulling a large trailer to back into a nearby campsite. It was not going well. A woman, whom I assumed was the wife of the driver, was standing at the back of the space waving her arms. Whatever these hand signals meant they were being ignored by the driver. He had very little room to pull forward to get a proper angle for backing up. He stopped. He opened the door of the truck, got out and walked away, leaving the truck running and blocking the road. The wife noticed all of us watching.

"He'll be back. He walked off so he wouldn't really lose his temper and start yelling."

"Meanwhile," George said, "he's blocking the road."

"Not much I can do about that," said the wife wearily, as if she had been in this situation before.

"If I can make a suggestion," said Angel, "my dad is an expert at backing up trailers—"

"A man doesn't usually drive another man's rig," George protested.

"Just this one time?" said the wife. "I would really appreciate it."

Just then an RV came to a stop on the blocked roadway. George went over and explained the situation to the driver who was angry and did not want to wait for the other driver to return.

"Okay. I'll do it," said George. "Jack, you stand in front and help me pull up within six inches of that tree. Angel, you stand in the space where I can see you in the rearview mirror and don't make any hand signals unless I'm going to hit something."

It took a couple of tries but it worked. When the husband returned ten minutes later, we did our best to ignore his astonishment. After he joined his wife in the trailer Angel said, "She should tell him she did it all by herself."

Our shared laughter led to some easy conversation. We talked about being on the road, about campsites, about how great it was to be American. I mentioned that I planned to take the next day off. I thought I saw Angel and her mom exchange a glance. We were silent for a moment. I felt I was expected to say something. George said he had noticed my fishing pole and I confessed that it was a way to start conversations. Then he asked what my biggest challenge had been so far. I told them about the donut. I laughed with them and as I laughed, I realized how seldom I made fun of myself. It felt good in an odd sort of way. (Allison often told me I was too serious.)

George asked me if I missed my family. I finished the last of my pie and coffee before I answered. "Not as much as I expected, so far." This was true sometimes and not true other times. I would be riding along and all of a sudden feel lonely. Other times I was happy to be away from them. Also, I guess I didn't want to admit to Angel that I was lonely. "There is so much going on," I added. "Riding the bike, being out in the world."

Angel said, "I'm going to college in ten weeks and three days. I love Mom and Dad, but I can't wait to get away on my own. I want to ..."

"Prove yourself?" I offered.

"Yes, exactly," Angel agreed with a big smile. "I plan to go pre-med. With a minor in drama."

I knew what was coming next. Ariel asked me about my plans.

"I'm not sure. I like being outside. Maybe ski instructor in the winter and river guide in the summer. Or maybe college. I like American history."

"Well, Jack, you don't have to decide right away. On your solitary trip you have some thinking time," said George.

"I like to just sit and think. All the way through high school, I felt I didn't have the time."

"I sometimes wake up in the middle of the night and can't get back to sleep so I think, and think, and I still can't see why the world is the way it is, wars, poverty, all that," said Angel.

"I didn't know that you ... I wish you had talked to me," her mother responded.

"Why? The world is changing so quickly older people can't keep up."

"Jack, do you agree with that statement?" Ariel asked.

"Ariel, don't put our guest on the spot," George said. "Jack, Angel is going to college on a full scholarship. She's the smart one in the family!"

"Maybe she's smart enough to come home after she graduates and explain the world to me," Ariel said.

That statement made for a prolonged silence. I was busy thinking about asking Angel to spend my day off the bike with me, but I was nervous about asking her in front of her parents. I almost said the heck with it and went back to my tent, but Angel was smiling and looking at me.

"I think you are enjoying your freedom," she said.

"All the way to Denali," George mused. "Long way."

"Three hundred miles a day," I said proudly.

"Iron butt? Starting tomorrow?" George asked.

"Off the bike day tomorrow, but, yes, no more donut."

"A toast," George said, raising his coffee cup. "To the iron butts among us who get things done. Definitely a good quality to have, Jack, as you go out into the world."

During my trip so far, I had talked mostly to adults, which wasn't a bad thing, but now I really wanted to spend time with someone my age. I wanted to spend time with Angel.

"Speaking of a day off," I said. "I'm planning to ride the gondola and do a hike on the summit and if Angel is interested, could she go with me?"

"You ask me, not my parents," Angel said.

I looked at her. I looked at her parents. "The answer is yes," Angel said.

"Well," said George after exchanging a look with his wife, "I consider myself a good judge of character and you seem like a reliable young man, so if you promise to be safe, no climbing snow fields or petting grizzly bears, I don't see why not."

I thought he saw George wink at his wife, but I wasn't sure.

"The bugs are coming out. Let's call it a night," said Ariel. "Breakfast is at eight. Join us and I'll pack the two of you a lunch."

"That is very kind of you, thanks," I said.

"You're welcome," said Ariel.

The next morning was a perfect early summer mountain day. Angel was ready to go when I went next door. She was leaning against the RV in a patch of sunlight with her eyes closed and a smile on her face. She looked angelic. We had breakfast inside the RV, then filled Angel's day pack with water, lunch and extra clothes. The gondola ride would top out at seven thousand feet.

After we boarded the gondola, I mentioned that Angel's parents had seemed almost eager to be rid of her.

"They were ready for some privacy."

"Really?" I replied rather stupidly.

"Yes, really. My parents are into each other. Romantic. We have only been on the road ten days, and they signed me up for two ranger-led walks that they didn't go on."

"So that bit about my good character was ...?"

"Total baloney. How about your parents?"

"Yea, I guess."

"I mean do they really like each other? That seems more important than, I don't know, young, crazy love."

"My parents don't always get along. They argue about money. My dad smokes. Last year we remodeled the garage into a bedroom. I live out there mostly. When I get home, I'll be paying rent and my share of food costs."

"Amazing they let you go on this trip. Maybe they wanted to be alone for the summer?"

"Maybe. I was a little surprised. Do you have a young, crazy love back home?"

"Let's just stay with today," Angel answered. "Look. We are almost at the top."

The sun was above the eastern ridge, but at this altitude, the light wind still had a bite. We decided to check out the Wildlife Interpretive Center before our hike. Angel seemed to know a lot about animals. At each exhibit, she had something to add. We stood in front of a stuffed grizzly bear for a long time. "Stuffed wild animals make me sad. They take something dead and make it look alive. It's like a trick."

I didn't know what to say. I was thinking how big and dangerous it looked. I wondered how brave I would be in front of Angel if we came across a real one. Outside on the deck, we pulled jackets out of the pack and set off across the ridge. I tried not to think of anything except being on this mountain with a new friend. Besides taking a day off from riding, I wanted to take a day off from thinking. Angel must have read my mind. She said, "We are so lucky to have this day in the mountains away from everything else!"

I agreed but wondered why it was so hard to not think about something. I spent a lot of time in my high school classes "lost in thought" as they say. It was a good thing my parents insisted that I get all As and Bs. And here I was again, on a mountain, thinking about school. I told myself to pay attention. "Seize the day."

Angel had a plant identification book with her. She often stopped to check out individual flowers or shrubs. She told me a science teacher at her high school had turned her on to botany. "Plants are far more complicated than you might realize."

"Really? Why?"

"Look at sunflowers. Every day they turn to follow the sun. Or these tiny alpine flowers? They know their chances of survival in a harsh environment increase if they hug the ground."

"They know? Do they have brains?"

"It's more likely evolution."

"Enlighten me."

"Over thousands of years, the flowers that grew too tall didn't survive to make another generation while short ones did. Dandelions do the same thing, but, like every day."

"What?" I asked, dumbly.

"There are dandelions in the yard. You mow the lawn—"

"Hundreds of times, half the houses in the neighborhood—"

"This is how smart dandelions are. After being cut off for being tall, the same flower doesn't grow as tall. They're fast learners."

"And I didn't notice! So how old is this individual flower?" I asked.

"That's a great question. I might have to research that when I get home. There are also flowers that generate heat and melt their way through the snow."

"That's cool."

"To us, it's a peaceful, beautiful day but all around us plants and animals are competing for limited resources or watching for predators. To us, a hawk in the sky is a thing of beauty, but I bet a ground squirrel sees it differently," Angel added.

"Whoa, ease up. My head is spinning."

"Oh, I imagine your head is doing fine. There is so much to look at, to understand. Are you sure you don't want to go to college?"

"And what? Major in everything?" I said with some annoyance. "Sorry, but everyone at home has been telling me to 'go to college.' It will still be there if I put it off for a year or two. Besides, I have to pay my own way."

"I'm sure you could do it ..."

"Today, remember?"

"Okay. Look at all that is going on here within ten feet of us! Not just flowers but ground cover, microorganisms in the soil and lichen on the rocks. The lichen is slowly eating the rock."

"Eating the rock?"

"Sure. With acid. It just takes a lot more time than for us to eat our lunch, but Mother Nature has all the time in the world."

"Unlike us," I said.

"We have today. Time is the world. Time and forces below ground lifted these mountains inch by inch."

"Time and glaciers carved the mountain valleys," I added.

"Time and evolution created the man and the woman now sitting on this mountain top having a great day and the language to talk about it."

Unlike solitary Mt. Shasta, the mountains here seemed endless. The lake below sparkled in the sun. The alpine meadow at our feet was crowded with wildflowers. The sun was just warm enough. There seemed to be a pause in time. We hiked for another hour. I tried not to think but simply appreciate where I was. After all, just a few short weeks ago I had been in a stuffy classroom struggling to get a "B" in Algebra II. Today was so much better I could hardly believe my good luck!

We stopped for lunch. Angel took binoculars from the pack. "Want to take a closer look at the ski runs?"

I consulted a trail map I had taken from a rack at the base of the lift at the visitor center. The double black diamond trail on the far ridge looked seriously steep. "I love to ski," I said.

"I believe it. You seem excited just looking. Maybe you could be a ski instructor?"

"I've only been skiing four years but last season I helped teach some sixth graders from my school. I liked it."

"I volunteered at our local hospital. Didn't like the hospital atmosphere."

"I thought you were going pre-med?"

"That's to please my mom—she dropped out of medical school to have me. Also, it gives my dad bragging rights. I'll probably change after my first year."

As I scanned the ridge opposite us, I spotted something brown moving out of the trees. "Bears!" I exclaimed. "A sow and a cub!"

"No way."

"Here, Angel," I said, handing her the binoculars.

"Hey, another cub came out of the trees. They're wrestling. They're chasing each other. One just ran under its mother. Now the cubs are wrapped in a bear hug and rolling down the hill."

"Very funny." I took out my camera, but the lens wasn't strong enough for a good photo. I snapped off a few frames anyway and took a picture of Angel looking through the field glasses without her noticing.

"Now it looks like the mother called them back. Oh, Jack, I can't believe it. It's lunchtime. You know? They're suckling. Here. Have a look. Life!" For several minutes we handed the field glasses back and forth watching the bear family.

"Lunch is over. They're moving off ... might go behind the ridge ... they're gone," Angel said.

In unison, we both said, "That was unbelievable!" Laughing, Angel added, "Something to tell our grandchildren about."

We hiked until we reached the edge of a snow field. The sun was now quite warm. We spread out our jackets and laid down, not quite touching, in the shelter of a rock. I was soon half asleep and sensed Angel was as well. The warmth of the sun was exactly right until clouds covered the sun and a cool wind came scurrying across the ground. I opened one eye and sat up. The western sky was full of thunderheads. I tapped Angel on the shoulder. "It looks like we might be in for an afternoon shower."

"Brrr," said Angel. "But that was very nice my friend Jack from Mt. Shasta City, California."

"Which is a long way from Madison, Wisconsin," I said.

We looked at each other. I leaned toward her for a kiss. She tousled my hair and said, "Jack. Take a deep breath of this mountain air. It will clear your head."

Instead, I said something stupid. You know how it is, sometimes, just before you say something stupid, an alarm goes off and you just kind of mumble. In this case, my words were as clear as the mountain air. What I said was, "But my lips are lonely."

The words hung in the air between us. Angel laughed first, a small, coughing kind of laugh. Then I laughed. Then our laughs became one giant, hysterical laugh. We would almost stop, then laugh again. We finally stopped when a family of hikers came by. We packed up and headed back to the gondola.

On the return ride down, wind rocked the gondola and rain spattered the glass, but by the time we reached the lower terminal, the sun was out again. On the way back to camp, we stopped at a store so I could buy postcards and something for dinner. Angel had already told me that her parents were taking her to a fancy restaurant at the lodge that night. Another heavy rainstorm moved in as we reached the campground. Angel asked me to wait while she ran inside.

When she returned, she said, "I don't expect you to show up in Madison any time soon, but here's my address. Please send me a postcard when you arrive safely at your uncle's."

"I can do that."

"We had a great day together!" And with that, she was gone. I threw a cover over my bike and retreated to my tent for my dinner of a deli sandwich, chips and coke. After dinner, I continued reading *Annapurna*. Very scary. I'm not sure if this book encouraged me to climb mountains or discouraged me.

It continued to rain. I decided to write in my journal. I actually had two journals; the one my mother gave me and one I had purchased at a visitor center. The one my mother gave me was for my report on the trip to go along with photographs when I got home. Show and tell. The other was for my private thoughts, or thoughts I might share with Davie or maybe Allison. I had only talked to my parents on the phone once so far. Sharing the trip after it was over was one thing but as it was happening …

I turned to the other journal. I had trouble writing anything because my thoughts were unfinished, like a house being built. Questions. I had a lot of questions. Which made me think of Mrs. Grady, my high school history teacher. I mowed her lawn every summer for years. When I finished, she would invite me in for a coke (a drink my mother did not allow in the house) and a conversation that started slowly with town news would usually end up being about the meaning of life or the state of the world.

Questions like where did we come from? If there is only one God, why do we have different religions? What is love? Why are there so few democracies in the world? Is happiness all that important? Questions that seemed bigger than my brain, but I enjoyed talking to her. Some of the same questions had come up during my solitary ride. I decided when I got home, she would be the first person I would talk to after my parents.

I managed to turn off my headlamp just before falling asleep. When I woke up, I could tell that the rain had stopped. I looked at my watch: midnight. I unzipped the tent flap and looked out; no lights on in the campground except at the bathroom. Not a cloud in the sky. The Milky Way, not quite solid white, but more stars than at home. I tried to go back to sleep. No luck. I dragged my pad and sleeping bag to the picnic table. With my head on my folded Carhartt jacket, I looked up at the stars and, much to my surprise, the northern lights! I had heard you could sometimes see them in June at Banff National Park. To the north beyond the trees, faint but fluorescent waves of green light danced.

I remembered I'd seen a meadow off the trail to the lake. I hoped it would be completely dark there. I rushed to my tent, grabbed my boots and headlamp, and ran—afraid I would miss them. I stood in the middle of the meadow, turned off my lamp and looked north. The green in the waves was unlike any green I had ever seen. It looked like something from out of this world. It was joined by pulsating bands of purple and pink. The northern lights, or aurora borealis, happen when charged particles from the sun collide with gaseous particles in the atmosphere. I watched until they faded away, wondering if I was the only one in the campground to see them. I wished Allison could have been with me. I wished Angel could have been with me. Okay, that would be awkward.

What a day! I walked back to camp a happy man.

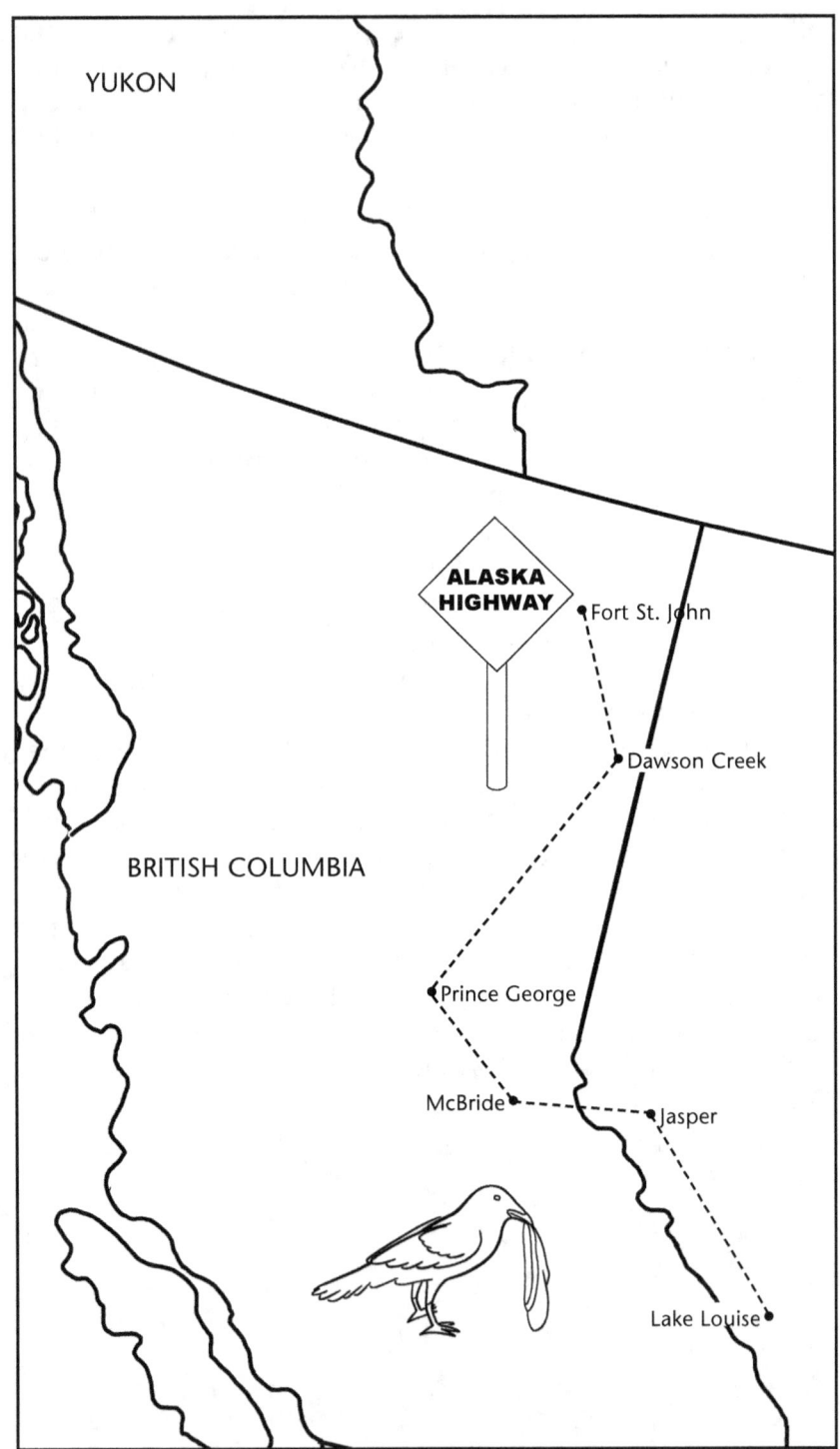

YUKON

BRITISH COLUMBIA

ALASKA
HIGHWAY

Fort St. John

Dawson Creek

Prince George

McBride

Jasper

Lake Louise

Chapter Four

Unexpected Encounters

At first light, I was jarred awake by the call of a Steller's Jay, also known as a camp robber, on the picnic table next to my tent demanding a free breakfast. I looked over to Angel's trailer. No signs of life. I decided to get an early start. Before anyone else was up, I walked to the nearest dumpster and threw away the donut. After a pre-breakfast of leftover Oreo cookies, a juice, and a banana, I went over the daily checklist for the Honda. I checked the tires for abrasions and proper pressure. I checked the oil level, lights, and just looked closely at everything. I tightened a screw on a cover plate that seemed to need tightening every other day. I looked over at Angel's campsite. Still no signs of life.

I started up the bike and left the campground as quietly as possible. Near the summit of Bow Pass (6,700 feet), I spotted a group of big horn sheep. I used the zoom lens on my camera to get a closer look. From a park brochure, I learned that the bighorn had come to North America from Siberia ten thousand years ago over a land bridge. At one time, there had been millions of them, but now the population was reduced to thousands due to disease and overhunting.

I watched as they zig-zagged up the cliff, needing only a few inches of rocky ledge to stand on. One male (I could tell by the large, curved horns) jumped a twenty-foot gap just as I clicked the shutter on the camera. I was using the camera more and more to gain an understanding of what made a good photograph. On the hike with Angel, I had taken several shots of just rocks and flowers.

I continued north on the Icefields Parkway. Both sides of the road had vistas of mountains as tall as 12,000 feet with hanging glaciers spawning fast-flowing rivers green with glacial runoff. I stopped to admire the Columbia Icefields and the Athabascan Glacier. Both were practically next to the road. There was little traffic. I was near the northern end of the three-thousand-mile-long Rocky Mountain Range stretching all the way south to New Mexico.

I stopped at the village of Jasper for breakfast. When I left the cafe, there were a half-dozen people standing around my bike taking pictures. "What the heck?" I rushed over. The largest crow I had ever seen had unzipped a pannier and was busily throwing my underwear and tee shirts onto the pavement, apparently looking for food! I shooed the bird away. A few of the onlookers complained they hadn't gotten a good photo. I ignored them.

"I guess crows grow bigger up here in Canada," I said to a man standing beside me as I picked up my clothes.

"That's a raven," the man said. "Bigger than a crow, smarter, larger curved beak. I've been coming here for years. Before they modified the trash cans, one raven could hold it open for another one to go in, then they would switch places. I've even seen them work together to carry off a day pack."

"At least he didn't fly away with my underwear," I said.

"I looked them up on the internet," the man continued. "One scientist, just for fun, taught a raven to put money in a vending machine and select a snack."

"You're putting me on," I objected.

"No. How about this one. Scientists placed a narrow cylinder, partly full of water, with food on a floating board too far down for the raven to reach. Beside the cylinder was a pile of small rocks. The raven—"

"No way," I interjected.

"Yup, the raven dropped pebbles into the cylinder until the water floated the board high enough for him to reach the food."

"Yesterday, it was flowers," I mumbled. "Today, it's ravens."

"What was that?"

"So basically, I'm walking around thinking about animals or birds one way and it turns out I have completely underestimated them."

"Not really 'seen' them is how I think of it. Every time I visit, I join as many ranger-lead walks as I can. I'm always learning something surprising."

"That seems to be the theme of my trip so far," I said.

"How far are you going?"

"Denali National Park. To work for my uncle. I'm on a schedule but on the way back in September, I'll take more time to explore."

"And hope you don't get snowed on."

"Thanks, happy trails!"

As I rode away, he called out, "Good luck with the fishing!"

Headed northwest on Canada Route 16, shortly after leaving Jasper, I crossed from Alberta into British Columbia. About five o'clock, I felt a steady wind from the southwest pushing against my left side. It grew in intensity. It looked like it might rain. I had little experience riding in rain or wind and I wasn't sure how much to lean the bike. The wind grew stronger. Trucks going in the opposite direction created a brief lull in the wind, throwing me off balance. "Be one with the bike," I said to myself, but the bike didn't seem to be in agreement. The sky turned a frightening black and the rain pounded down.

My mechanic had coached me for these conditions: reduce speed by ten miles an hour, anticipate curves, increase following distance, and avoid strong braking. I was grateful that my father had bought me new tires. I held on, constantly wiping the rain off my face shield. Just as I was starting to feel halfway confident, a passing truck sprayed me with a sheet of water. For a moment, I was riding blind. I was surprised I didn't crash. A few minutes later, I reached the town of McBride. A flashing motel sign appeared out of the gloom.

"Tough out there," said the clerk. "Side winds are tricky."

"Plus getting nearly drowned by passing trucks. You ride?" I asked, looking at the motorcycle tattoo on his forearm.

"Harley. Only on sunny days. Weather looks good for tomorrow. There's a washer and drier by unit six if you want to dry your clothes, do some laundry."

"Thanks." I was looking forward to a hot shower and a real bed.

That night, I called my parents. I thanked my mother again for the camera and told her I was now in the habit of looking for possible photos other than landscapes. I assured my parents that all was well; that I was happy, the bike was running fine, and I missed them. I hung up wishing, not for the first time, that my friend Davie could have joined me on my adventure.

Morning dawned bright and sunny. I felt clean and rested. There was one small detail that bothered me. In Canada, passing bikers gave a salute that was different from the American salute. A slight twist of the wrist maybe? I felt I never got it quite right.

About ten o'clock, after three hours of peaceful riding, I rounded a corner and braked to a halt. My first steel cord bridge. I had heard horror stories. The metal bridge looked about two hundred feet long and it looked wet from last night's rain. There were uneven steel cords running the length of the bridge, spaced about the width of a motorcycle tire. I couldn't turn back or go another way. There was only this road north.

I remembered the advice another rider had given me, "Don't go slow!" At a slow speed, trying to keep the bike balanced could be tricky. The front wheel might kick out. I knew that any motorcycle is more stable when accelerating. Knowing it and doing it were two different things. I pictured myself hitting the bridge at twenty miles an hour, then steadily accelerating until I reached the safety of the far side.

"I can do this," I said out loud, and then I did. I pulled into the gas station just beyond the bridge.

"Good job," said the attendant. "Some riders go too slow and fall over."

"How many more of these things are there?" I asked.

"Between here and the start of the Alaska Highway, just two. After that I'm not sure."

"If it had been raining, I think I would have walked the bike across."

"That would be embarrassing. There you go, all set, for what, another hundred miles?"

"About that."

After lunch in Prince George and another steel bridge, I headed north on Highway 97 hoping to reach Dawson Creek and the official start of the Alaska Highway. A campground just south of Dawson Creek was full so I turned up a gravel logging road and found a meadow next to a small stream. I washed off in the creek and went to bed early. The farther north I went, the more stars there seemed to be in the sky. I felt good. I felt that I was truly north. Back home, temperatures would be nearing a hundred.

After a good night's sleep and an hour of riding, I reached Dawson Creek and the Alaska Highway.

The original, gravel Alaska Highway was built during the summer of 1942 by the U.S. military in response to Japanese threats to shipping lanes during World War II. It provided a land-based way to supply military bases. Building the road across unsurveyed territory in such a short time was considered an engineering miracle. Over the decades, most of the roadway has been paved.

I parked my bike in front of the sign and took a photo of it. Then I asked a stranger to take a photo of me on the bike. It was still over fifteen hundred miles to my uncle's lodge! Back on the bike.

As I came over a rise, I knew something was terribly wrong, but it took a second for it to completely sink in. At the bottom of the hill, a truck had left the road and smashed into the bridge abutment. I pulled the bike over to the side of the pavement. I told myself that I needed to do whatever was right. To stall for time, I took off my helmet, jacket and gloves. I looked up and down the road hoping that someone would appear. No traffic. No sign of help.

Even though I felt that no one could be alive in that pile of crumpled metal that had been a truck, I knew I had to investigate. I looked up and down the highway again. Nothing. I could see a man behind the wheel. He looked as crumpled as the truck. Grateful there was no fire and knowing it was stupid, I called out from a distance, "Hey Mister, can you hear me?"

The man looked dead, but I wasn't sure. The door was jammed. A log truck pulled up.

"What the hell? Step aside, Kid." I hadn't realized I was holding tight to the truck to keep from fainting.

"If you're going to be sick, get it over with. I might need help."

"No. Later maybe. Tell me what to do."

"We have to get the door open. I have tools in my truck."

He came back with a Peavey (a long-handled logging tool with a point and a hook made for rolling logs), a sledgehammer, and a first aid kit.

"No cell phone service. We're on our own." He slipped the hook over the inside of the door and we pulled on the tool with all our strength for what seemed like forever. I felt that the muscles in my shoulders were about to shred when the door popped open, throwing us to the ground.

"Damn! It worked," said the logger. "Can't get the seat belt loose, feels like the buckle is smashed. Take that bear knife of yours and see if you can cut him loose." (Mostly for show, I traveled with a hunting knife on my hip.) The logger stepped aside, his hands covered in blood. I forced myself closer. The steering wheel had punctured the man's stomach. I cut the part of the seatbelt nearest to me. We twisted the man free of the steering wheel and pulled him onto the pavement. The logger put his hand on the man's neck. "I can feel a pulse." I turned away and threw up.

"I'm going to drive back up to the top of the last hill. See if I can get someone on the radio."

"You're leaving me alone?" I protested. He ignored me.

"Here," he said, handing me a first aid kit. "Take the roll of dressing and press it into the hole in his stomach. Hard. Might stop the bleeding. Can you do that?"

"Yes," I answered, almost choking on the taste of vomit in my mouth. I knelt next to the man without looking at his face, cut away his bloody shirt and, closing my eyes, shoved the ball of bandage into the hole. Finally, I heard the logger return. The man under my care convulsed and blood came out of his mouth. I looked into his terrified eyes, then he went completely limp.

"Police are on their way," the logger called out.

"It's too late, he went and died on me."

I stumbled down the bank to the river. I heard the logger call out that I had done the best I could. I walked knee deep into the stream. I took off my bloody shirt and washed it. I washed my hands and arms. I scrubbed at my pants with sand. Over and over, I splashed water on my face. Hearing a siren, I climbed back up the bank.

The body was covered with an emergency blanket. The policeman asked me questions and I heard my voice answering. When he was done, I asked "Who was he?"

Looking at his notes, he said in a flat voice, "Steve Johnson, age forty-two, I know him slightly. Married to Dorene Johnson. No children. A gold miner. I heard he was going bust."

"I looked into his eyes. All I saw was fear."

The officer and logger didn't say anything for a minute.

"Are you going to be all right, Son, on the bike?" the officer asked.

"I think so," I answered.

"Okay. Mrs. Johnson might want to write you. To thank you for trying to save her husband. Can I give her your address?"

"I guess so ... wait, I'm not sure I want my parents to know ... my mother worries about accidents, she might be curious, open the envelope. Here's my uncle's address in Alaska," I said, handing him a business card.

He made notes and handed back the card. I walked to the bike. I put on my helmet, heavy coat, and gloves very slowly.

The logger approached me. "I live about forty miles north. If you want to camp in our backyard, have a home cooked meal, I'll tell my wife to expect you. There's phone service in about ten miles." When I didn't say anything, he added, "We help each other out, here in the north country."

"Thanks, I'll keep riding." My voice sounded choked.

I rode almost to Fort Nelson thinking about nothing at all, finally stopping at an unappealing, treeless, gravel campground next to the highway, half full of weather-beaten recreational vehicles. Most of the blood had been washed away by the cold water of the river, but I needed a shower and a change of clothes. After paying more than I wanted to for the night, the man in the office directed me to the coin-operated laundry and showers. Suddenly, I was very hungry. The shock was wearing off. I bought two sandwiches, chips, cookies and two cokes for dinner.

While my clothes were in the machine I swam back and forth, back and forth, in the short, heavily-chlorinated, lukewarm pool. I wished it were a clear mountain lake. I wished I could swim until I could no longer even imagine the smell of death. I was angry; angry that I had been the one holding the dying man in my arms without being able to offer him any comfort.

When I took my clothes out of the washing machine, the blood stains were faded but still there. I put them in the dryer anyway. If only, I thought, Davie had been able to come with me, I would not have had to face this encounter with death alone. With a shaking hand, I dropped several quarters into the pay phone. Davie answered just as I was about to give up.

"Davie! I thought you would never answer."

"How's the trip going?"

"Good. The bike is running great. People in the campgrounds are friendly. You wouldn't believe the size of, well, everything here in the north country. Huge valleys, mountains everywhere."

"Something is wrong. Your voice is strained and don't tell me it's the connection."

I told him about the fatal truck accident.

"I'm sure, Jack, my friend, you did everything you could. The images will stay with you for a while … at the moment he died … they say you can see or feel a person's soul leave the body."

"All I felt was terror and nausea. I kept closing my eyes."

"God was with you."

"Maybe. Tell me some local news. I'm feeling a bit lonely."

"I ran into your mom at the grocery store. She told me to tell you to call more often. My dad and your dad have joined a forty and over slow pitch softball team. It isn't pretty to watch. The Haskins boy? The one who's taken over your lawn mowing customers? He lets the grass get too long. The neighborhood is looking seedy without you."

"How's work on the bridge going? Has everything you welded stayed welded? The bridge hasn't fallen down?"

"It's going okay. The boss is always telling me to go faster. The way the guys at work talk bothers me—all that swearing. My first paycheck, with overtime, was more than I want to say out loud. And now for the big news. I'm in love!"

"Anyone I know?" I asked.

"Alice Bagley," answered Davie. "I met her at church. She was here freshman and sophomore years, moved away, just moved back last week. A redhead."

"Skinny little thing?"

"Not anymore."

"Love at first sight?"

"No sarcasm, Jack. This could be IT!"

After we hung up, I thought to myself, I have been gone just a week and already the world back home is changing. I retrieved my clothes from the drier and settled down in the tent to read. No luck. The sights and sounds of the day kept coming back to me.

Shortly after eleven, the sun dropped below the horizon and a deep twilight settled over the land. From the hills on the far side of the highway, a wolf howled. "The call of the wild." A second wolf answered. I crawled out of the tent wrapping my sleeping bag around me. The wolves howled back and forth. From across the drive, a man came out of his trailer also wrapped in a blanket. The rest of the encampment slept on. The wolves went silent. Back in my tent, I was unable to get comfortable. My shoulder muscles were sore from freeing the injured man. To distract myself, I pictured myself skiing; skiing an easy trail, in a rhythm, like music.

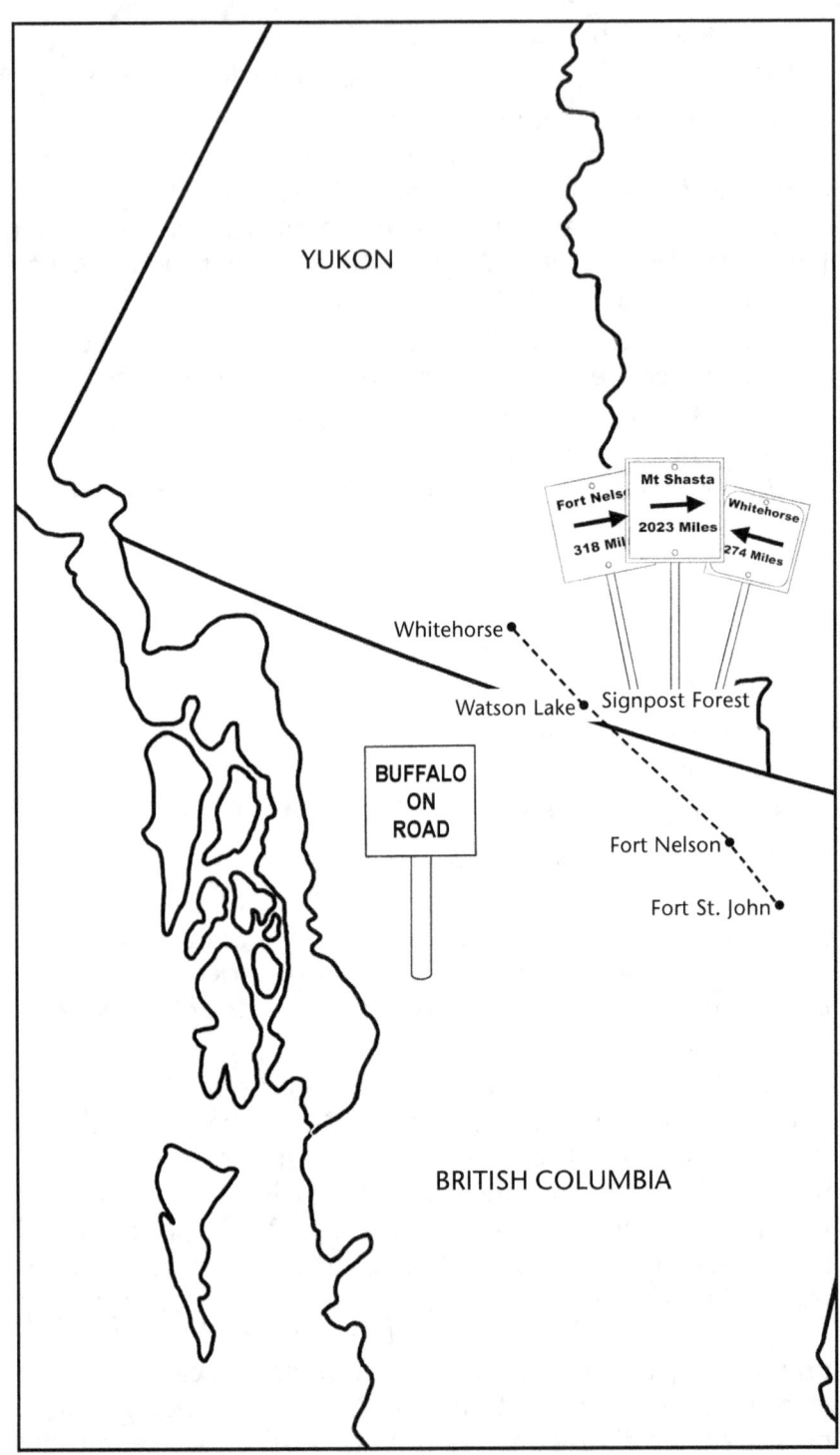

Chapter Five

Not So Crusty Old Man and Others

The next morning, I woke to the sound of the pickup and trailer next door pulling out of the gravel driveway. I boiled water for instant coffee, added a left-over chocolate covered donut, a hunk of cheese and an apple for my breakfast, then checked over the bike and I was ready to go, hoping for an uneventful day.

About noon, when I pulled into the parking lot of the Lone Wolf Café and gas station, I noticed an older Toyota pickup with a camper shell and a snazzy-looking homemade trailer tightly packed with what looked like machine tools and a brand-new high-end dirt bike guarded by two husky-looking dogs. Sitting at an outdoor table was a sparse, elderly man of medium height. He called out, "Hey, motorcycle man, join up here."

As a change from heating up canned food or convenience store take out, I sometimes ate two meals a day in restaurants around eleven and four if I could time it right. I'd noticed that the farther north I went the friendlier people seemed to be. "Sure, just let me hit the john, wash up."

"Susie will take your order inside, bring it out. I recommend the wild caught grilled trout, salad and fries."

After placing my order, I sat down at his table with a large homemade chocolate milkshake. The man was clean shaven, dressed neatly in Carhartt pants and a plaid wool shirt.

"I'm Daryl, from Upper Michigan, going north. I just retired from being a machinist. Built the trailer there."

"Jack, from Northern California, northbound to Fairbanks."

We talked motorcycles and hot springs on the Alaska Highway. My order arrived. While I ate, Daryl explained that he had just turned sixty-five, collected his first social security check, signed over the house to his younger brother who would take care of their mom, loaded up the pickup, attached a trailer to it full of tools and a homemade horizontal sawmill, and headed north.

"Great trip so far except the Canadians held me up at the border for two days because of my guns, fourteen of them."

"Sounds like you are ready for anything," I said.

"Yup. Bears, rascals, gov'ment agents, whatever turns up at my homestead. Flew up here a month ago, bought some land outside Haines, hauled in a trailer. Plan to live in the trailer while I build a cabin. Know what the secret to survival is up here?"

I barely got in a "No, Sir," before Daryl continued.

"Do what you need to do first, then what you want. That, and never let yourself think about giving up and going outside to the lower forty-eight. Follow me?"

"Hmmm," was all I managed to say around a mouthful of trout.

"Good, isn't it?"

"Best meal of the trip! So, you're going to be a mountain man? Live off the land?"

"Not like your romantic idea of it, I guess. I'm old. I've made concessions. My stake is only two miles from town. It's on the coast. Not as cold as the interior. I can snowshoe into the post office if I have to. I've rented shop space, plan to do a little machine work, lunch at the senior center, fish and hunt, live in the woods and be part of the town."

"Sounds good."

"Now, take my cabin. It will be just sixteen by twenty feet, floor and ceiling heavily insulated, efficient wood stove. I have it all figured out."

"Won't it be lonely?" I asked. Daryl gave me a quick look but ignored the question.

"I'm a machinist. I make things down to a thousandth of an inch. Precise. My goal in coming up here is to live precisely how I want. Off the grid. And away from the grind of what we laughingly call civilization. No electricity except solar panels to charge batteries in the summer, a small generator in winter.

"Arctic nights?"

"The stars and the northern lights. Might get two more dogs and train them all to a sled. No TV, no internet. I plan to send and receive mail. Hunt, fish, gather food in season. Take my guitar playing to a new level. Maybe meet an in-town lady. I saw that look, Jack. Never too old for love. I'm giving myself two luxuries; a propane-powered refrigerator and a propane water heater. I plan to stay clean. I will never be a grizzled old man. Also, I recorded two hundred hours of classical music. Do you listen to classical?"

"I'm not much of a music person."

"You have to, dammit, or your life will be incomplete. What I'm saying here is, the world has way too many rough edges, bad times, imperfections. But with classical music, the greats, Beethoven, Mozart, Bach, and Chopin being my favorites, there are passages that are so perfect, they restore your faith in humanity. You came on this trip to learn things, right? Well, I strongly urge you to listen to classical music when you get home—you don't have to analyze it— just listen to it the same way you might listen to the woods. Ever do that? Hike into the woods, go off trail, sit down, don't move?"

"Well, kind of, I guess," I answered, thinking of my night alone in the woods back home.

"This isn't a 'kind of' situation. You have to commit to silence. First thing, the birds will come back. People have no idea how many birds they scare away when they walk down a path. Why I've had birds practically land on me, had deer walk right by me—wild turkeys even. Why? Because I was sitting perfectly still. Are you listening or thinking about getting away from this old maniac?"

"Some of both, but mostly I'm listening."

"Take riding your bike. I bet sometimes you feel in sync with the bike and sometimes not so much."

"That's true. Sometimes it goes too far. An old biker warned me about bike euphoria. You're so in tune it's like you're floating down the highway; feel like you're not really moving, like you could step off the bike. Then it's time to stop and take a nap."

"That's true, a natural high won't get your chores done. You don't do drugs, do you? They are just a substitute for the real thing."

"No."

"Or smoke? The cigarette companies put nicotine and other chemicals in the tobacco to make all smokers addicted. Smokers are drug addicts, pure and simple."

"My dad finally quit last summer. I grew up around his smoke. Not going to happen with me."

"Well, enough of my ranting and raving. You finish up and I'll introduce you to my travel companions. Best trained dogs ever. Just with hand signals they'll do whatever I ask them."

Before walking over to the truck, I ducked back inside the restaurant and thanked them for my meal.

When Daryl opened the truck door, the dogs jumped out and immediately obeyed a hand signal to sit down. "Jack, meet Sandy and Charlie, my grizz early warning system." Both dogs shook hands. "I can hike through the woods, and they will never be more than ten feet away and immediately heel at a hand signal."

"They sound like great friends to have."

"How are you going back, Jack?"

"Back home? I hadn't really thought about it. I have a whole summer ahead of me."

"My brother, the banker, and his wife took an Alaska cruise. Talked about it for years, but instead of the cruise ships, I heard the state ferry system is great. Store your bike below. Sleep on deck. It leaves from Skagway, next to Haines. Here's my name, post office box. If you make it to Haines, go to the post office, they'll explain how to find my place. You can tell me your stories and I can tell you mine. I'll throw a few venison steaks on the grill, we can watch the bald eagles, dozens of them."

"I might just do that," I answered. "My mother bought me a camera. I was wondering, could I take a picture of you and the dogs? Sitting on the tailgate maybe?"

I looked through the viewfinder. I waited. I clicked off a few frames. Waited. Clicked off a few more. I felt I had captured something. I showed the pictures to Daryl.

"Wow. You pressed the button at just the right moment on this one. After you get home can you mail me a hard copy—memory of being on the road?"

"I promise."

A few hours later, I turned off the highway to get gas at a marina. I decided to take a quick swim. Due to the long days of sunshine, shallow lakes near the Alaska Highway were not freezing cold. They were just cool enough to be refreshing. After my swim, I was getting ready to leave when a float plane landed and taxied to the dock next to a large pile of boxes. The pilot waved me over. "I'm making a short trip to a village. It's a half hour each way. Help me load the plane and you can go along."

"It's a deal."

"Just leave the bike in front of the marina office. It will be safe."

I had never been in a plane. When its pontoons broke free from the lake, it was a great feeling. Fly like an eagle! It felt like escaping from school on the last day of the year. It was like pointing my skis downhill on an intermediate trail and just letting go. Fly like an eagle!

As we flew north, in the distance stretched mountain after mountain. A panorama! I had never seen anything like it. "There are places in those mountains where no one has ever been," Jim, the pilot, told me. I believed him. On our right were forests and lakes and one lonely looking road— my road.

Every day the tremendous scale of the north blew me away. Yesterday, I had stopped at a roadside kiosk that had a map of the valley I was riding through. To me the mountains looked about ten miles away but, according to the map, they were fifty miles away. The valley I was riding through was a hundred miles wide.

There were waves on the lake when we came in for a landing. It was rough. The plane bounced a few times. Jim looked unconcerned. "Any landing you walk away from or, in this case, swim away from is a good landing," he said. We motored to the dock where a reception committee was waiting. Bush planes were the village's only connection to the outside world. Everyone helped unload and we were off again. Halfway back Jim asked me if I wanted to fly the plane. On his controls, he showed me how to go up, down, and gently turn. I then copied him on the co-pilot's controls. I told him it seemed easier than riding a motorcycle in traffic—nothing to hit!

"It is easy," Jim said, "unless there's a white out or you are struck by lightning, or encounter extreme turbulence, get lost, run out of gas or there are moose on the runway. Up here it's only you, the beautiful earth, the plane, and God. No one can help you." I didn't know what to say. God was a subject I didn't talk about much.

"If the engine stops, how long can this plane glide?" I asked.

"Probably not far enough," Jim answered. I thought about his answer. I asked myself how cool I would be in an emergency. Maybe not cool enough. I didn't ask him if he had ever crashed.

After we landed, I took a picture of Jim standing next to his plane looking happy and proud, the same way I always feel standing next to my motorcycle. It was still running great. On lonely stretches of highway, I often didn't see anyone else in either direction for thirty minutes or more. It did feel like it was just me, the bike, a beautiful world, and maybe God.

Shortly after arriving at a campground south of Watson Lake, I went next door to introduce myself to a fellow motorcyclist. He was one of those skinny Harley guys that look as tough as nails but not healthy. I was surprised he didn't have a pack of cigarettes rolled up in his shirt sleeve.

Before I could say anything, he pointed to his license plate which read—SOLO.

"I ride solo and whatever it is you're after, I'm not interested."

I retreated. On the other side was a family of three. The wife was one of those people who just looks happy. The dad was a very fit man in his forties, and I could see that their son had Down Syndrome. There had been a Down Syndrome student at my high school. At the beginning of the school year, he had been harassed by a small group of students. That had ended when the captain of the football team sent out the word that Steven was his special friend and anyone bothering Steven would have to answer to him.

"We're going down to the playground to shoot hoops. Want to join us?" the man asked.

"Sure. I'm Jack."

"Allen, and this is Matthew."

"I'm Rebecca," his wife added. "You guys go ahead. I have chores to do."

At Matthew's urging, we all shook hands rather formally and walked to the court. Surprisingly, the basket had a net and the rim wasn't bent. Matthew had his sweet spot, about eight feet away and to the right, which was perfect for a bank shot. Allen was one of those people who was easy to talk to. And I learned that he was an emergency room doctor.

After passing and shooting informally, Allen suggested to me that we play some one-on-one with Matthew as the referee. I was dubious but Allen assured me that Matthew knew what he was doing. "See, I have my own whistle," Matthew said, pulling it out of his pocket and giving it a loud blast. It turned out Matthew was a good referee. He even called his dad on charging. I lost by eight to ten but enjoyed the competition.

After the game, I asked Allen if we could talk about the fatal truck accident. Matthew went ahead to help his mother make s'mores. Telling the story this time, I remembered more details. It still wasn't easy. I still felt bad that the man had died.

"It sounds like you did everything you could. You weren't driving the truck, he was. Maybe he fell asleep for a moment. You said there was little traffic. Maybe he had been bleeding for some time before you got there. Using the Peavy to get the door open was clever. I've lost patients. It happens. It haunts me, especially the children. Sometimes when I walk out of the hospital, after many hours at the operating table, and it's a beautiful sunny day, I feel that I never want to go back."

"To the blood and guts?"

"You get used to that. To the life and death. The responsibility."

"But you do."

"I have a skill and a passion. It is necessary that I go back."

"And you believe you can do it better than anyone else."

"Very perceptive. You're right."

"I keep meeting people on this trip who are sure of themselves. I'm not sure what I want to do. Last winter I was passionate about skiing."

"I have a feeling you will find your way. Let's see if the s'mores are ready."

We joined Matthew and Rebecca at the campfire. We talked about our travels. Well, their travels. Every year Allen volunteered for Doctors Without Borders while his wife and Matthew also traveled abroad.

"One thing I can't get used to here," said Rebecca, "is how it doesn't get dark until midnight. We don't really need a campfire."

"When I get to Denali, it won't get fully dark at all."

"I can think of a few things you can't say in summer in the far north," Allen said.

"Really? This should be good," said Rebecca.

Matthew had moved on to roasting marshmallows. He very carefully toasted each one a golden brown.

"The prisoner will be shot at dawn. Under the cover of darkness."

"Wait until dark," Rebecca added.

"The stars are out. It's darkest before the dawn," I said.

"You can't say, 'I'll meet you at the lake to watch the sunset,'" Allen added.

"It is going to be such an adventure for you, Jack," Rebecca said.

"I should make enough for a season pass and new skis and put something in my college fund."

"We're skiers. Well, Rebecca and I ski and Matthew snowboards," said Allen.

"I shred big time," said Matthew in a loud voice. "If you come visit us in Colorado, we can shred together!"

"That would be great."

"We live outside Fort Collins," Rebecca explained. "Arapahoe Basin is our home ski area. Matthew is training for the Special Olympics."

"Gold medal here I come!"

After we finished our s'mores, I stood to head back to my campsite for the night. "Allen, thanks for the basketball game. And letting me talk about the accident."

"It will stay with you for a while."

"Good night."

"Have a safe ride," said Allen.

"See you later, alligator," said Matthew, grinning.

"In a while, crocodile," I said and turned to go.

"Not so fast, Buster," said Rebecca. "In this family, we hug."

"Me, first," said Matthew, hugging me in a strong bear hug. Allen pried him loose to make way for a four-person hug. It felt good. Rebecca walked me back to my tent.

"Matthew loves getting postcards. I bought some national park ones at the store. When you get to Denali, could you mail one to Matthew? I wrote in the address."

"You bet."

The next morning when I got up, all was quiet next door. I guess I had hoped they would invite me over for breakfast, but no luck. After a breakfast of an apple and two candy bars, I hit the road.

A short time later I was at Watson Lake, gateway to the Yukon Territory and the site of The Sign Forest: over 80,000 road signs donated by travelers since 1942. From the bottom of my pack, I took out an aluminum sign for Mt. Shasta City, California, that Davie had cut with a laser at the end of our school year, and added it to the collection.

I wanted to catch a show at the nearby Northern Lights Center, but time was wasting and I had three hundred miles to cover to get to Whitehorse, Yukon Territory.

Chapter Six

Are They Friendly?

After two uneventful hours, I rounded a curve only to quickly brake to a halt. I had seen a sign earlier warning of buffalo herds on the highway and here they were! About fifty of them; bulls, cows, and calves milling around completely blocking the road. Some were grazing on the sides of the road, some seemed to be socializing and others, napping. I turned off the bike, took out my camera and studied the buffalo through the telephoto lens. I had never seen beasts so noble and so ancient looking. I had the keen sense that this was their land—the highway being a minor inconvenience—and had been for thousands of years. I also thought that if humans didn't make it as a species, the buffalo would still be here.

They looked calm. I waited. Fifteen minutes went by. They still blocked the road. I hoped a car would show up going in my direction and I could follow them through. Another five minutes passed. They still looked calm. I snapped a dozen photos, put the camera away and waited.

A gap near the center of the road opened. I took a chance. I started the bike, put it in neutral and coasted down the hill toward the herd. The animals seemed unconcerned. I eased forward. They shifted about. I was almost in the clear when a big bull, looking all of his two thousand pounds, snorted and turned to face me. The space on each side of the bull was blocked by other animals. The bull rolled his massive head and stared at me.

I wondered if I should shut off the bike. The bull snorted again and took a few menacing steps forward, then stopped. I looked into his eyes from ten feet away. "Wild animals are supposed to be afraid of people," I said to myself, but what I saw in this animal's eyes was a complete lack of fear.

47

I realized this animal could kill me if he wanted. I was glad he was a vegetarian. I decided to ignore him. I looked at the sky. I pretended to be indifferent. The patriarch stamped his feet again but instead of charging, he turned away. I shifted into first gear, rode safely through the gap, and was on the road again. Whew! I got away with one there.

A few miles down the road I had another scary moment when I heard a siren and saw flashing lights in my rear-view mirror. I pulled over and took off my helmet. A trooper approached. "I came over the rise back there while you were in the middle of the herd. Do you realize that was dangerous?"

"Yes, Sir. I do now."

"Normally, if I turn on the lights and the siren they scatter. I didn't dare do that with you in the middle of it all pretending to be a buffalo or whatever. License and insurance, please … California. You've come a long way."

"I have a job waiting for me at my uncle's lodge south of Fairbanks."

"I could give you a two-hundred-dollar ticket for harassing wildlife, but I have a feeling you will never do it again."

"No, Sir. I promise."

"Good thing you're not on a Harley. They hate the sound of Harleys. Last summer a big old bull knocked a guy off his bike then trampled it. Have a good trip."

"Thank you, Sir."

I pushed on to Lakeside Campground. After a meal of canned sardines and peaches, I rode the bike to a marina on the far side of the lake and decided to rent a canoe. The young lady running the rental shop was an Athabaskan native named Tanana. We talked a bit, you know, just teenagers saying, "Hey?" but she seemed shy.

"Let's get you set up. One life jacket. Two paddles in case you lose one. It happens. And a whistle in case you're drowning or lose both paddles. Be back in an hour. That's when I go home."

I paddled around the lake, enjoying the change of pace from being on the motorcycle. I now always carried my camera with me. Tanana was standing at the end of the dock.

Using the telephoto lens part way, I took a photo. I stopped to inspect a rounded beaver den. I lay back to photograph a circling bald eagle. I let the canoe drift. When the sun went behind a cloud there was less surface reflection. I photographed underwater reeds swaying in a current.

I drifted and closed my eyes, felt the sky above me, breathed in the smell of the water, the smell of the forested shore, and listened to the lap of water against the canoe. I fell asleep. After what seemed just a few minutes, I heard a whistle. Tanana was waving me in. I paddled back and helped her stow the canoe. "Thanks," she said. "I'm done for the day."

"I've been taking photos of people I meet along the way. Can I photograph you?"

"You already did. From the canoe."

"Not a closeup. I liked the dark outline of you and the dock."

"Go ahead. Steal my soul."

I assumed she was joking. But on the other hand, my photos of Angel and the man at the café did seem to capture something of who they were. I looked at the photos I had taken of Tanana. They seemed to be incomplete. Maybe it was a matter of trust.

"You're trying to decide if I'm good looking, aren't you?"

I stuttered something in reply.

"I've seen that look before."

Tanana's high forehead, rounded, strong cheeks and her honey brown skin made her different than anyone I had seen before.

"But that's okay. I can't tell if you are handsome or not."

We laughed and that broke the tension between us.

"My granny says I'm beautiful. Boys like me. I look in the mirror and it looks like me but isn't me. Just a reflection of me. No complaints. I see other girls here, or at the store where my sister works, wearing make-up, eye stuff. What are they doing? Trying to make up some new story about themselves?"

"I never thought about it that way."

"My sister brought some eye stuff home for us to try. My mother caught us. I thought we would be punished but she just laughed until we washed it off. Here, our faces are the same Athabaskan faces as always. We came here over the land bridge from Russia ten thousand years ago. Our faces are outdoor faces. American girls have indoor faces."

"Do you ever want to leave the village?"

"I went to Calgary once for a basketball tournament. This fall I'm going to college there to be a nursing assistant. Then I will help the one doctor we have here. I'm not afraid. My family, village will be with me."

"You have a big family?"

"Parents, one grandpa, one granny, three brothers and sisters, aunties—too many sometimes. You?"

"No grandparents. They all died when I was young. Uncles, aunts, but at home just my parents and me."

"We are having what is called a 'cross-cultural conversation,' aren't we?" Tanana said, sounding tired. "It would be hard to really get to know each other. Athabaskans talk differently. Less direct."

"Still, I've enjoyed talking with you. And you are beautiful."

Laughing, she answered, "Maybe yes, maybe no."

"Can I give you a ride home?"

"I don't think so. Granny would not approve. It's only two miles. I run through the woods to get in shape for basketball season."

"Aren't you worried about bears?"

"Bears are my spirit animal. One would never harm me. I suppose your motorcycle is your spirit animal."

"For now, maybe. The pictures I took? They don't really look like you. How about I stand over there and you run by me?"

We did. And the picture of an Athabaskan Girl Running was a good one.

Chapter Seven

Life

My day was going well until I made my second driving mistake of the trip. On a motorcycle, the rider must watch diligently for several hazards: debris on the road, which can seem to appear out of nowhere if one follows too closely the car ahead, potholes just wide enough for a motorcycle wheel to fall into, cars changing lanes too quickly or changing lanes without seeing the bike rider, oil patches, and in the national parks, oncoming drivers crossing the center line while looking at the scenery.

Before my parents had allowed me to get my motorcycle license, they had signed me up for a two-day motorcycle safety course taught by a retired motorcycle policeman. We all rode medium size Hondas supplied by the state, even the few Harley owners who had been sent to the class by insurance companies. I had been the youngest rider there. I survived the obstacle course, the written exam, the emergency stop test, and the emergency turn drill which is what saved me from serious injury after crossing a bridge and being confronted by a right-angle turn that I was definitely not expecting!

Had there been a warning sign I didn't see? I had crossed the bridge at about forty miles an hour. Unable to stay in my lane because of my speed, I was on a collision course with an oncoming car! As I had been taught in the class, without thinking about it, I pressed down hard on the right handlebar, forcing the bike to dip and swerve to the right, missing the side of the car by less than two feet! There was a suspended moment when I looked into the terrified eyes of the woman driving the car. The bike wobbled but didn't go down.

I pulled over and looked back. The car had turned and crossed the bridge. My heart was thundering and sweat broke out on my forehead. I took off my helmet and breathed in a lungful of sweet air, wishing there was some way I could apologize to the woman driving the car. I thought of going back to see if there was a sign I had missed but decided that, no matter what, I was responsible for my own safety.

After stopping twice for quick naps in town parks and eating a large pizza dinner at about four in the afternoon, I arrived at a campground near Whitehorse at ten o'clock. I found a sheltered campsite on a wooded side hill. The camp below me was empty. Somewhat weary of the road, I heated water on my camp stove, took a quick sponge bath, shaved, and soon fell into a deep sleep.

My sleep was disturbed around midnight by the sound of quarreling voices; teenage voices, one boy and one girl. The boy's voice sounded drunk and demanding. The girl's voice was mocking and resisting. They were both using a lot of swear words. That was something Allison and I had never done. I felt that I should cough, or something, to let them know I could hear them, but I hoped they would just go away.

I had seen my school's production of Romeo and Juliet. Romeo's wooing of Juliet was loving, witty, and heartfelt. This boy's way of wooing was the opposite. He repeated rumors about the girl's behavior which she profanely denied. I supposed that the boy was asking to be loved but in a way that could not possibly work. I was undecided if I should do anything until the boy's tone of voice became threatening.

I put on my pants and stepped out of the tent. I went to a gap in the bushes overlooking their camp. The two were face to face. The boy was holding the girl's arm. I tried to make my voice deeper. Which didn't make sense because they could see me in the half moonlight. They could see I was their age.

"Is there a problem here?" I demanded.

The girl twisted her arm free. "The only problem is this jerk won't leave me alone."

"Let her walk away!"

The boy hesitated. The girl struggled free and ran shouting and swearing. The jerk and I now faced each other. Ten feet apart. I felt I should say something about not getting drunk, about not assaulting women, but I just wanted to go back to bed.

"I'm guessing I outweigh you by thirty pounds. I'm sober and you're drunk. It's time for you to call it a night."

"She agreed to go for a walk with me!"

"Yes, a walk," I said, trying to define the situation.

"You are such a loser."

"Maybe, but you will never win the lady fair by being ... violent."

"Whatever, Dude." With that, he walked away.

I went back to my tent still pumped with adrenaline. I hadn't been in a fight since seventh grade. At six feet and one hundred and eighty pounds, I supposed guys tended to leave me alone. From their conversation, I guessed they went to the same high school and came from well-to-do families. I didn't understand why they talked to each other the way they did. I didn't want to think about it. I only wanted to sleep.

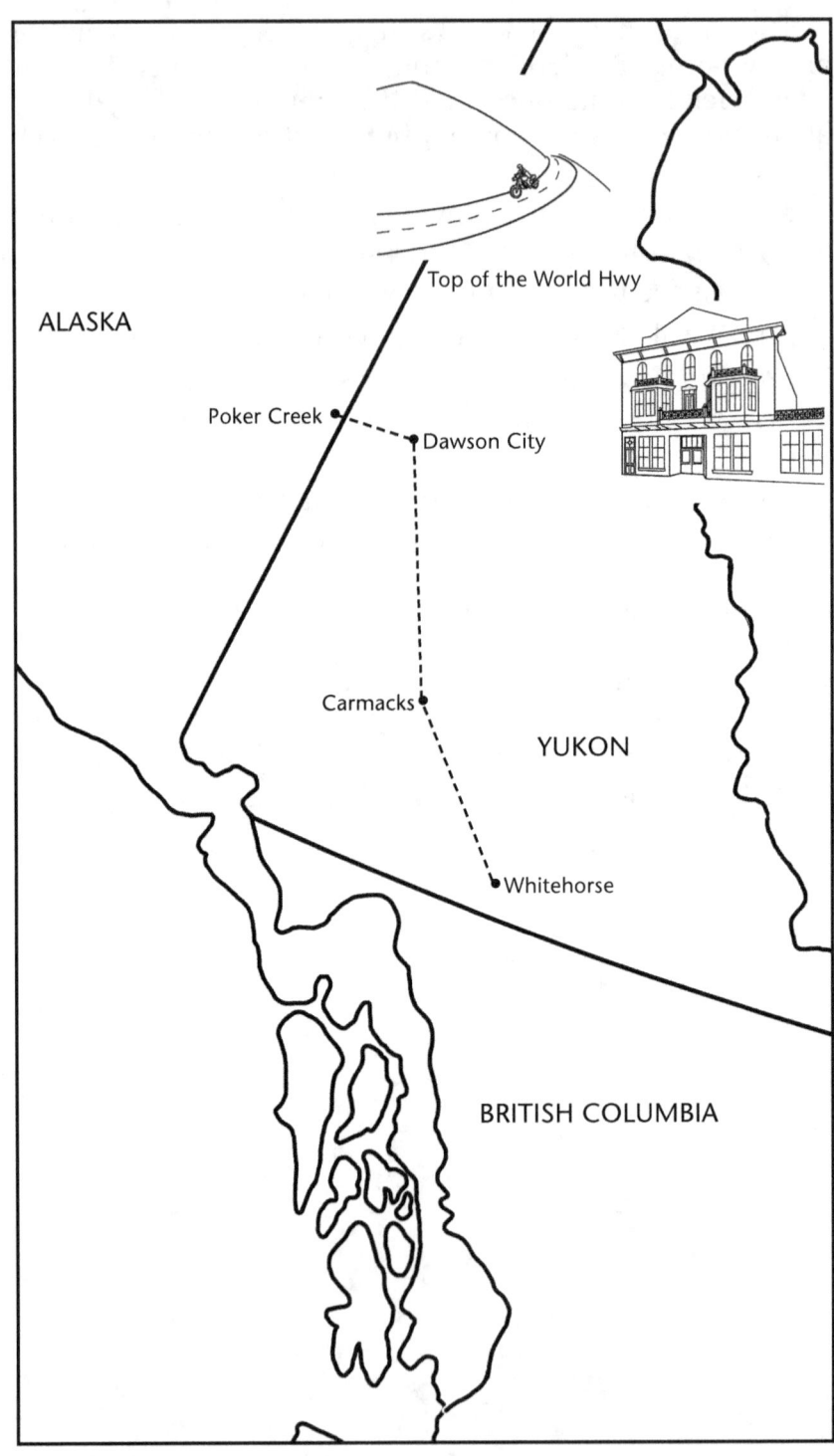

Top of the World Hwy

ALASKA

Poker Creek •
Dawson City

Carmacks •

YUKON

• Whitehorse

BRITISH COLUMBIA

Chapter Eight

Gold!

I woke up at five with the remains of a dream about the confrontation of the night before still in my head. I needed to be at my uncle's lodge in three days. Looking at my map while eating a breakfast of a bagel, banana, and a cup of coffee, I decided to turn off on Route 2 north of Whitehorse to Dawson City and the Top of the World Highway. Dawson City had been the center of the great Yukon River gold rush in 1898. A few easy days to finish my journey is what I needed.

For the first time on the trip, I felt like I had plenty of time. A map at the campground bulletin board showed a four-hour hike around the lake. I decided that was just what I needed to clear my head. It worked.

Back on the road, I stopped at Takhini Hot Springs for a soak, then Pelly Crossing for gas and lunch and arrived at Dawson City, Yukon Territory, about seven. The sun was still high in the sky. I felt too tired to camp out. I checked into a motel, stood in the shower forever, ate a large steak dinner, was in bed by ten, wrote in my journal, and fell asleep.

I slept until eight. A deep sleep without dreams. Sleeping in a bed made me feel a little homesick. I should have called my parents the night before but had felt too tired. I called but got my mother's voicemail. I took another shower and shaved. I picked up a tourist brochure at the front desk. I planned to camp that night at the town of Chicken, Alaska, which was only a three-hour ride from Dawson and my last camp out of the trip. The town was named Chicken because the gold miners could not agree on how to spell "ptarmigan," a local, chicken-like bird.

Gold Fever in the spring of 1898. The idea that an ordinary man could become rich made people quit their jobs and leave their families for Seattle. Thousands of gold seekers, adventurers, scam artists, dance hall girls and businessmen filled ships in Seattle headed north. *Gold!* Free for the taking! For some, it turned out to be true. Most came for gold, but others came to make money off the miners. Boarding houses, laundries, dance halls, restaurants, and even an opera house sprang up as if by magic.

After breakfast at the Klondike Kate Restaurant, I joined a downtown walking tour and spent the morning visiting the Palace Grand Opera House, the Danoja Zho Native American Museum, Diamond Tooth Gerties Gambling Hall, and the Jack London Cabin and Museum. After dining again at the Klondike Kate Restaurant, I was ready to hit the road.

I crossed the Yukon River on a small ferry and traveled west on the Top of the World Highway which followed the crests of a series of ridges. I was at the edge of the Arctic to the north and on the edge of civilization to the south. This was as far north as I would be on this trip. I wondered what the northern lights would look like from this vantage point. I thought about some of the milestones of my trip so far: my acceptance of solitude on the bike, my satisfaction at the end of each day, the incredible scenery, the people I had met, and I felt more … open than when I had left home.

I pulled into a picnic area and took out a package of fig newtons and my thermos of coffee. The scope of the view was greater than anything I had seen on the trip so far. Sky and earth. A land almost without people. In its own way as vast as the stars. Something was different, but I couldn't figure out what it was. Then it hit me—in the vastness of the view, I could sense if not actually see, the curve of the earth! My planet! My earth! With its oceans, mountains, forests, and prairies seemed … fragile … a sphere floating in space, protected from annihilation by a thin layer of atmosphere. How lucky I was to be here at this moment. I wished Davie and Allison could be with me. Would their excitement match mine?

I was having what my high school history teacher, Mrs. Grady, would call an epiphany. My understanding was that an epiphany is when your senses or your thinking are altered by something extraordinary and unexpected. The world, your world, will never be the same. I took photos knowing they would not be enough. I dug out my journal knowing that words would not be enough but determined to try anyway. I just threw words down on the page. My coffee turned cold. My cookies went uneaten. I wrote until I had no more words. I felt heroic.

I mounted my trusty steed and pressed the starter. When the engine came alive, I felt a surge of anticipation and happiness knowing that more adventures waited for me.

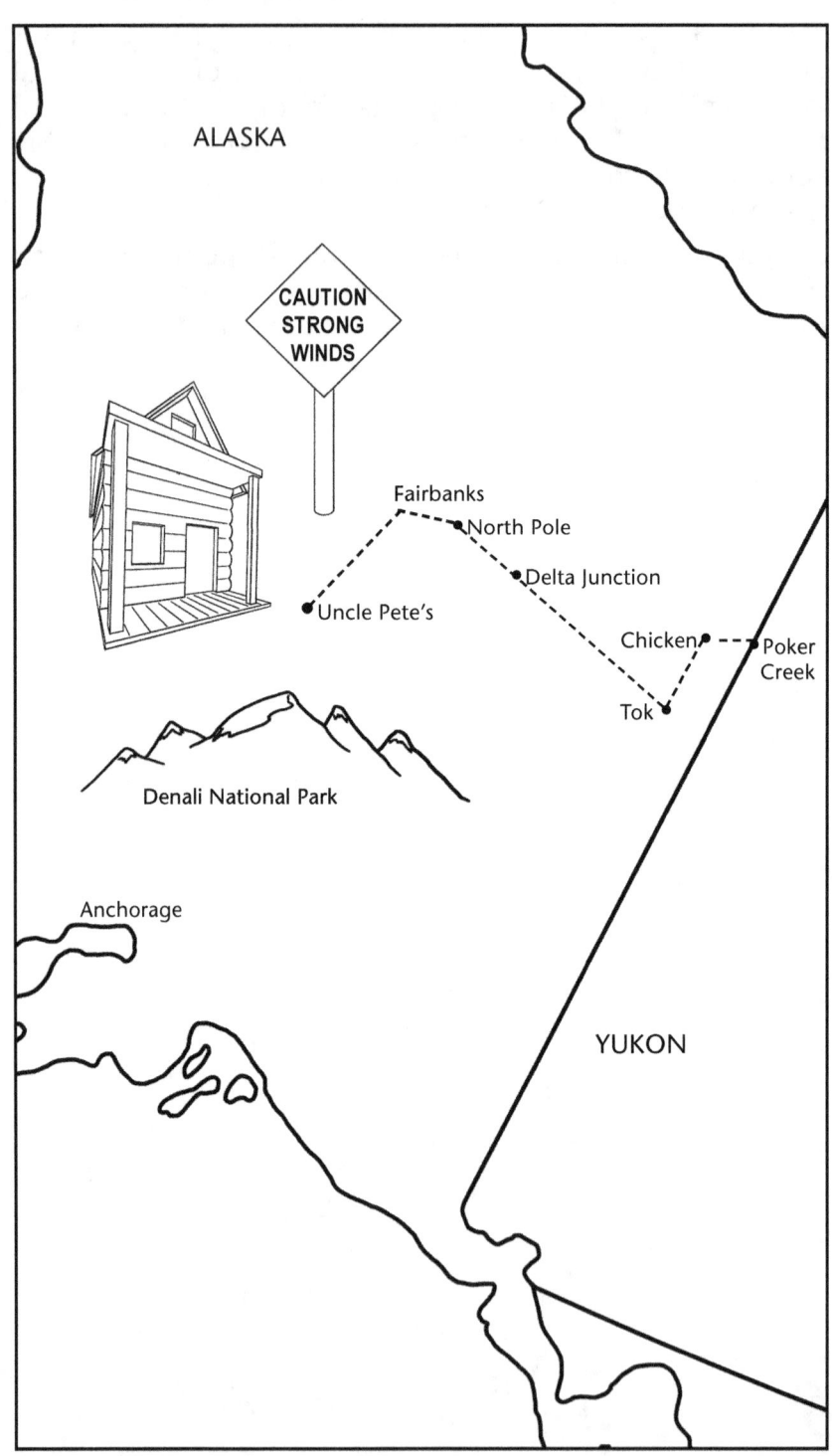

Chapter Nine

Entering Alaska

At Poker Creek, I crossed the border into Alaska. A homecoming. I stopped for a chicken dinner in Chicken, Alaska. Chicken is an active gold mining town without electricity, internet, or cell phone service. Instead of checking into the campground, I decided to push on so that the next day, my final day on the road, would be shorter. About ten I pulled off the highway onto a logging road and made a rough camp.

At Tok, Alaska, I turned west. Later, I had lunch and took my bike to a car wash at Delta Junction. I skipped the town of North Pole, skirted the city of Fairbanks, and headed south to my uncle's lodge and Denali National Park. I had called him from Whitehorse, and he assured me he had enough work for two "boys." I planned to arrive at dinner time.

At first, it was barely noticeable as gusts of wind slightly rocked the bike. Then it started blowing harder than what I had experienced during the early days of my journey. At first, I felt confident in my riding ability but it became a battle, a battle I wasn't a hundred percent sure I could win. Fear. Distracting fear. Lean the bike but not too much! The wind blew dust under my face shield and into my eyes. I didn't dare let go of the handlebars to wipe it away. Next, it started blowing gravel from the side of the road onto the pavement. Then it stopped gusting. Instead, it became a continuous force that changed angles as I drove around curves. It seemed unfair since I was only an hour from "home."

Then I saw a sign that truly frightened me. Caution. High Winds on Bridge.

I pulled over. I simply lacked the courage to continue. The wind made two different roaring sounds as it passed over and under the bridge. The sounds mixed together promising disaster. I considered turning back and looking for a place to hunker down, but I didn't want to disappoint myself. And my uncle was expecting me. I braced myself just to stay upright. A tree branch banged against the bike. I almost fell over getting it disentangled. I thought I could use the "start slow and accelerate" technique I had used on the steel cord bridges earlier in the trip to safely cross. But I wasn't sure. I tried to imagine slicing through the wind like a knife. It didn't help. The fear inside me grew and grew.

Suddenly, stronger than the wind and the fear, there was a voice inside me. A voice I had never heard before, a strong voice that forced me to listen. It said, "Get out of the way you fool before you get us killed!" The BIKE accelerated. The BIKE leaned sharply into the wind. I was inside the wind. The wind made it hard to breathe. The wind twisted my helmet, making it hard to see. The BIKE felt like it was both falling over and being supported by the wind. I thought I would never reach the other side.

Then we were across! The road turned away from the canyon. I could hear the motor. I could hear my labored breathing and feel my heart beating. I was alive! Tears of gratitude washed the dust from my eyes.

A few miles down the road, I pulled into a parking lot to catch my breath. A man was standing next to his RV. There was a crease down one side from the front wheel to the back.

"The wind pushed me across the bridge and bounced me off the guardrail. Please tell me, son, that you didn't ride across that bridge."

"I did."

"That's impossible."

"Beginner's luck, I guess." There was no way I was going to tell him about The Voice.

A short time later I arrived at my uncle's lodge and looked down at the odometer, 3,242.2 miles! I gave my bike's gas tank an affectionate pat for a job well done. Uncle Pete was tying up a boat at the dock. He waved and charged up the hill. My Uncle Pete—big man, big gestures, big smile. "Jack!

My boy! Welcome to Alaska! It's great, isn't it? No place like it in the world. You're going to love it here!"

He wrapped me in a bear hug and pounded my back. My "Thanks Uncle Pete, glad to see you," seemed small in comparison.

"Three thousand miles by motorcycle. What a trip that must have been. We just got our phone service restored. Call your parents."

"Yes, Sir."

"You missed dinner, but Mrs. M will fix you something, show you your room, whatever. She runs this place. I have a poker game to get to."

With that, he rushed off to the lodge. I followed in his wake, somehow feeling smaller than I had on the bike. A summer of good-paying, hard work was what I needed, but I would miss being on the road.

I found Mrs. M in her office off the kitchen. I guessed she was in her sixties. Sturdy. Strict. Hard to imagine her slowing down. I could feel her appraising me as I introduced myself.

"I've saved some fried chicken, homemade biscuits, and green beans from the garden for you."

"You have no idea how good that sounds after camping and eating in burger joints for three thousand miles."

"The first couple of summers, Ross, my husband, and I drove up from Flagstaff, Arizona. We wanted to see some of the country. Now we fly up. I guess it took you some staying power to ride a motorcycle all the way here. The guests are great and the money's good, but be warned, it's going to take commitment to work here."

"I like to work."

"We'll see. There's a washroom at the far end of the dining room. I'll heat things up for you."

"Thank you, Mrs. M."

After a dinner worth working for, Mrs. M gave me my room key, bed linens, and my mail: four letters from my parents, one from Davie and one from Allison. My room was narrow, with a bed, a bureau and an overstuffed chair that had seen better days. The one small window looked out on the back of an equipment shed. The bathroom was squeezed into what once must have been a closet. Feeling a bit let down, I went out to the common porch for employees and sat in one of the Adirondack chairs with my mail.

My parents were doing well. My mother had been offered a job as soon as she finished community college. Davie's letter was mostly about his new girlfriend and how he was saving money to buy a Mustang. The unopened letter from Allison felt like just one sheet. I looked at the river. I watched a boat go by. I listened to my uncle's laughter from his place at a poker table on the porch of the lodge. The evening sun was still high in the sky. I moved my chair into the shade of an aspen tree. I opened the letter.

> *Dear Jack,*
>
> *I am sure you won't be surprised to receive this letter. I write with love as well as sadness.*
>
> *By the time you return from your Great Alaskan Adventure, I will be in college in Texas instead of Colorado. Texas State offered me a full scholarship. I plan to return to good old Mt. Shasta City for Christmas. I am very grateful for the four years we spent together—we were so good for each other. I am grateful that I never felt anything but respect from you. We have reached a time in our lives when we are going in different directions. I feel we should now acknowledge that we have no hold on each other. We should embrace our new lives and see each other at the holiday with new stories to tell.*
>
> *Reading this over, it sounds too formal so, really Jack, have a great summer! You're in Alaska! Have fun, meet new people, make money, be safe on the return trip. Write when you can. I will send you my new address when I get to college in August for orientation.*
>
> *Take care, love always, Allison*

On the road, I felt neither here nor there. Now that I had arrived, my life back in California seemed far away. Just a few months ago, high school felt like it would go on forever. Now, I had moved on. My friends had moved on. I thought of calling Allison, but felt I had nothing to say. I called my mother and left a voice mail saying I had arrived safely.

I took a shower. The water had a mineral smell, and the water pressure was lousy. Tired, but not yet sleepy, I went back out to the porch with my journal. A bearded man paddling a canoe pulled up to the dock. From a picture in the dining room of him and Mrs. M, I recognized him as Ross McKenna, Mrs. M's husband, and a legendary Alaskan fishing guide. I would soon learn that he was a profane, profound, whiskey-drinking, pipe-smoking, poker-playing outdoorsman and just a lot of fun. Ross's profanity or swearing never included the "F" word. It consisted of folksy terms like "son of a sea cook." Around the campfire, Ross was a master storyteller.

When he played poker with the guests, he never lost if the game went on for more than an hour. All his winnings went to charity. He refused to tell anyone his secret except to say he was good at reading people.

When he saw me sitting on the porch, he came over and introduced himself. I liked him immediately. We talked about my trip. I confessed I knew nothing about fishing. He puffed on his pipe. He looked sad. "We will have to find the time to educate you."

"Thank you, Sir."

"You can call me Ross."

"I'll try to remember."

"How well do you know your Uncle Pete?"

"Not well. He would stop in every few years. His 'hell-raising ways' made my mother nervous."

"Your uncle is an old school boss, and he will probably be extra hard on you because you're family. If he tells you to dig a hole, you should ask how deep!"

"I like to work," I said, laughing.

"Our other guide, Vincent, is someone you should get to know. He likes people okay. He's just someone who never speaks first. Heck of a guide and a photographer. Smart too. We get the Sunday New York Times here on Wednesdays. A guest usually gets about three quarters of the crossword puzzle then Vincent finishes it in ink."

"Thanks for cluing me in."

"Which brings me to the true boss of the outfit ..."

"Mrs. M?"

"You've got that right. Besides cooking, scheduling raft trips and airport pick-ups, she does the books, writes out the paychecks, and distributes cash from the tip pool. Do not make her unhappy."

"No, Sir."

Ross struggled out of the deep wooden chair like a bear with a bad back. "I'm headed over to the lodge to see if Mrs. M can rustle up some coffee and apple pie. Want to tag along?"

"Thanks. Then it's early to bed for me. I have to be at work at six."

Chapter Ten

First Day on the Job

Mrs. M was already at work prepping for breakfast omelets when I walked into the kitchen.

"Morning, Jack. Coffee. Apron. Wash hands. Make sandwiches. Then help serve breakfast. We offer four kinds of sandwiches—big sandwiches. The guests love them. I've made one of each kind as an example. The bags are labeled with the guest's name and type of sandwich. Go to it."

I was soon to become a Jack of all trades: dishwasher, janitor, yard maintenance worker, airport shuttle driver, boat stocker and cleaner, greeter of guests, fish cleaner, bait chopper, grocery shopper, shuttle driver for the drift boat, and van cleaner. It was going to be a summer of "Yes, Ma'am" and "Yes, Sir."

Twenty minutes into sandwich making, Mrs. M stood behind me tapping her palm with a spatula. "You need to work faster and smarter. Think about what you are doing. Save a second here, a second there. Make all the roast beef, then all the turkey. Don't switch around. Set up your workplace left to right."

"Yes, Ma'am."

While I was making the sandwiches, Uncle Pete, Ross, and a tall, thin man picked up their breakfast plates at the order window. Nobody was talking. I assumed the tall man was Vincent. He had a half smile that looked like it could quickly go one way or the other. They sat at the table closest to the kitchen. As soon as they finished, they left to get their boats ready. On the way out, Vincent stopped in the kitchen door. "Jack, isn't it? Welcome to the team."

"Thanks."

"That was a surprise," Mrs. M said. "Vincent is a bit of an odd bird. With guests, he only talks about fishing, wildlife, and photography. The photos on the dining room walls are all by him. Some guests ask for him summer after summer and often buy a photo as a souvenir."

"My mother bought me a camera for the trip. Taking a good picture is harder than I thought."

"I once asked Vincent for advice and all I could get out of him was this: 'Don't expect to keep more than one out of fifty pictures and get rid of cluttered backgrounds.'"

"I'll work on that. Ross says he's super smart?"

"He is. He has a degree in philosophy from the University of Colorado, something I only found out after knowing him for eight summers. And I swear he remembers the name of every guest that has been on the river with him. Remembering the names of guests is part of your job too, Jack."

When I finished the sandwiches, Mrs. M informed me I was ten minutes behind schedule, so I had only ten minutes for a breakfast of sourdough pancakes, bacon, eggs, and coffee. I was up to the task, finishing just as the first guests arrived. By tradition, guests served themselves coffee and juice and came to the service window to call out their order and table number. Mrs. M didn't write anything down!

My job was to deliver the meals to the right table. I was a little nervous, but people were friendly. After all, they were on vacation. After breakfast, Mrs. M retreated to an armchair in her office for a twenty-minute nap while I cleaned tables, swept, and mopped the floor. I was forbidden from running the noisy dishwasher until Mrs. M woke up from her nap.

"After you finish the dishes, check the bulletin board," said Mrs. M, rubbing sleep from her eyes like a child. "On the board is a list of chores, broken down into half-hour intervals, every day, for the rest of the month. Each group of guests arrives Sunday evening and departs the next Sunday morning. You drive them to the airport. After you get back you have the rest of the day off. Questions?"

"No, Ma'am."

"Later today, I'll introduce you to Clarence, our twenty-year-old, twelve-passenger van. For some crazy reason, that van is very important to your Uncle Pete. You will clean it every day, inside and out, including the tires. Detailed instructions are in the glove box. It will take you no longer than thirty minutes. After dinner, Pete will take you on a test ride."

"What happens if I fail?"

"Failure is not an option. Tell you what, during your lunch hour, we'll take it for a practice run. Ever driven a stick shift?"

"Some, my dad's truck. The motorcycle. Same principle."

"Your mother sent your sizes. I have three uniform sets for you and one pair of coveralls. You will iron one pair of pants and one shirt every night before bed. Switch to the coveralls for anything dirty. Any questions?"

"No. I looked at the bulletin board. I would not have guessed Uncle Pete was so well organized."

"He's not. I am."

The test drive in Clarence went well. I finished work at eight, nearly fell asleep at the campfire while Ross was telling stories, and fell into bed at nine. I had survived my first day on the job.

Chapter Eleven

Work and Play

On my first Sunday off I accepted an invitation from the saddle horse and raft operation down the river to join an employee volleyball game. Employees from five lodges showed up. In the first game, I found myself playing next to a redheaded, blue-eyed beauty named Rachel who was the head wrangler at her lodge. She was easily the best player on the court. After serving several aces she eased up. Her bumps to me were perfect but I had trouble scoring.

"You play a good defense, but your timing is off on your spikes," Rachel said.

Stupidly, I said, "Story of my life, my timing being off." Rachel responded with a quizzical look and a slight smile. After two more games, Rachel, looking bored, left, taking any chance of me asking for her phone number with her.

The next Wednesday I was told to take six guests to a "horse whisperer" demonstration. Ethan Butler's presentation was at a nearby lodge with a covered arena and seats for a hundred guests. Ross suggested that I pay close attention. "You can learn something about people from Mr. Butler."

Soon after I had settled into a seat in the back row, Rachel sat down beside me. I prayed I wouldn't say anything stupid. Before I could say anything more than hello, Ethan Butler, mounted on a buckskin horse of some kind, rode into the round ring and came to a stop at center stage.

"See that?" Rachel said. "No reins. He controls the horse with his knees and his voice. He's a genuine horse whisperer." I guessed that must be a big deal. If Rachel was excited about it then I was all in. I nodded. Ethan introduced himself and explained that his horse, Viceroy, was the dominant horse on the ranch. Ethan's helper brought a second, young, skittish horse into the ring. I glanced at Rachel. She was as pretty as I remembered her. Ethan dismounted. Viceroy immediately let the new horse know who was boss. He chased it around the ring and nipped it on the butt. Ethan let Viceroy take charge.

"This is Star, my pupil for the day. Star has never been ridden or worked with a line. Horses are herd animals. They recognize and need to know their place in the pecking order. Now that Viceroy has established who is boss, he will let Star approach him."

Which is exactly what happened. I glanced at Rachel again. She had forgotten about me. After giving the horses a chance to bond, Ethan led Viceroy out of the ring. "I'm going to take Viceroy's place as the head honcho on the ranch." Ethan approached his student carrying a switch. He snapped it near the horse's rump to encourage him to make several turns around the circular corral.

Next, Ethan drew a curved line across one third of the arena. Before making his "student" run again he asked the audience to make noise when Star was outside the line but go completely quiet when Star was inside the line. It didn't take the horse many runs around the arena to decide that inside the line was safer. Ethan let him come to a stop and catch his breath. Without taking her eyes off the arena, Rachel whispered, "You are going to see magic happen!" I remained silent. I was already feeling magic happening.

"We use a round corral so the horse will never feel trapped." Next, Ethan caressed Star from front to back, the way a mother would groom it. "He's showing signs of wanting to bond. I'm going to let him decide on his own." Ethan walked to the far side of the arena, out of the safe area where the horse was comfortable. He stood with his back to the horse. Star shifted about and huffed. He took a few steps toward Ethan. Ethan ignored him. Star approached slowly and stopped just behind him. Ethan ignored him. I could feel the tension in the audience. Rachel leaned forward and put her hand on my knee. I don't think she was aware of doing it.

Star decided. He took one more step forward and placed his head on Ethan's shoulder. Everyone seemed to exhale at once. We understood that this bonding of man and horse was something special; not just between the two of them, but it represented centuries of bonding between man and horse. I was glad Ross had told me to pay attention. I felt … moved. I felt that I knew more about, well, life than I had an hour before.

Rachel's eyes glistened and they asked a question of me. I nodded yes, yes, that I understood to some degree why Rachel was moved and why she loved horses. There was a quiet ripple of applause; an acknowledgment by the audience that they had just witnessed something extraordinary.

"There is still work to be done," Ethan announced. "I need to strengthen the bond between us so that the colt will let me put a blanket and saddle on him." The rest of the presentation did not get the attention from me it deserved. I was distracted by thoughts of Rachel. Would we see each other again? What could I say to her? When I realized that the whisperer might ride this horse, a horse that an hour before had never been ridden, I refocused my attention on the ring.

Ethan leaned over the horse, getting it used to having weight on its back. He let Star smell the blanket before putting it over him. Finally, after getting a nod of approval from his wife who, he explained, watched the horse's body language and had the final call as to whether the horse was safe to ride, he eased a saddle onto Star while talking in a reassuring manner.

I thought that the horse looked at the man as if to say, "I don't know what you're doing but I guess it's okay." I glanced at Rachel. She ignored me. Ethan walked the colt around the ring a few times, then put one foot in the stirrup and slowly lifted his other foot off the ground. The horse skittered sideways. Everyone now realized that there was danger here, that at the last-minute things could go wrong. Ethan swung his other leg over and slowly settled his weight on the saddle. The horse looked back at him but nothing else happened. The audience let out a collective sigh of relief. He talked to the colt and rode him around the circle a half dozen times. Each time, Star was more receptive to following directions.

The show was over. Rachel's wranglers clustered around her, excited and awed by what they had witnessed. She was leaving.

"Jack, are you off work every Sunday?"

"Afternoons, after breakfast and an airport run."

"Why don't you stop by our horse barn about four?"

"Okay," I called out as Rachel was swept away.

That Sunday, Rachel was waiting for me when I pulled up to the corral at the Broken K Ranch on my motorcycle. She looked great in her tight jeans and cowboy hat. She looked glad to see me. Summer in Alaska was looking better and better.

"We have twenty horses and two ponies. The ponies are for little kids."

"Since the only time I have been on a horse was at a county fair ... maybe ..."

"No, Jack, you're too big. This is your horse, Molly, the most easy-going horse we have. I expect you two to be good friends. Molly is our first Horse of the Month this year."

"Does she get a reserved parking space in the employee parking lot? I'm trying too hard, aren't I?"

"Yes. Relax," Rachel laughed. "We like each other. There's a photo of Molly and a bio on the bulletin board and she is guaranteed a ride every day. Introduce yourself."

"Introduce myself?"

I did my best. Called her by name. Told her my name and caressed her front to back like the horse whisperer. I didn't really mean it. I did it to impress Rachel. It seemed to work but I think Molly could tell I was faking it.

After a tutorial on how to saddle a horse, we set off on a ride. I didn't really understand why a horse, a large mammal, would let another mammal ride it. I kept these thoughts to myself. In places where the trail was wide enough, we rode side by side and talked about our families and our hometowns. Rachel was from Greenwich, Connecticut. I guessed her parents were rich. She was going to Barnard College in the fall for her sophomore year. A fancy private school.

"My parents worry about me being so far from home. It's annoying. One phone call a week seems like plenty. Do your parents worry about you?" Rachel asked.

"Yes. I don't know why. I've never done anything really crazy. You?"

"No. The party scene in high school didn't appeal to me. So, you're the 'Steady Eddie' kind?"

"If that's a good thing, then yes."

"It is for me."

We were in Alaska! Away from our parents! We rode without talking for a bit. It seemed okay. I shifted in the saddle. I did not need a painful reminder of my hemorrhoid donut days on the motorcycle.

"There's a small lake off to the right. I see a moose there sometimes," Rachel said.

"I've heard about them. Haven't seen one yet."

"We'll leave the horses here and walk in."

"Like Indians?"

Without talking, we treaded softly from tree to tree. We glanced at each other and smiled. We were having an adventure together. Near the closest shore of the lake, a bull moose was standing shoulder high in the water, plants hanging from his mouth. He seemed to be looking at us, but I wasn't sure. His funny appearance did nothing to make him seem less dangerous.

Rachel whispered to me, "Moose are mostly passive but unpredictable. Sometimes they charge. If he looks directly at us and his ears go flat, it is time to run."

"Like now?" I asked.

"Yes! Run!"

We dodged back and forth through the trees. The moose charged to the edge of the forest and stopped. We kept running until we were out of his sight. We arrived at the horses laughing and out of breath. We hugged. Briefly. Rachel broke away and mounted her horse. As we continued our ride on the narrow trail, Rachel talked to me over her shoulder. She told me that a moose could swim several miles and could dive to the bottom of a lake, hold its breath, and eat aquatic plants without swallowing any water. "That's why their head is shaped the way it is," she added. Somehow it hadn't occurred to me that moose were funny looking for a reason.

At the next open meadow, Rachel spurred her horse into a run. Molly seemed disinclined to go any faster than a slow trot, which was okay for me. So far, I much preferred my motorcycle to riding a horse. I felt that Molly didn't like me. Then it happened. Molly stepped on a yellow jacket nest! The wasps swarmed upward, stinging Molly on her stomach. Instantly, she became a bucking bronco. I had no idea what to do! Just before I was about to be thrown off, I dropped the reins and grabbed the pommel with both hands and squeezed Molly's side with my legs as hard as I could. Molly stopped bucking but took off like a rocket. My right foot came out of the stirrup. I hung on. It looked like the meadow would come to an end and Molly would be running full speed into the trees. I had a micro-second vision of being knocked off the horse by a low-hanging branch. I knew I needed the reins to stop her, but I was afraid to let go of the pommel. Desperate, I lunged for the reins. I snagged them and pulled back hard. As fast as Molly had been running, she was even faster at stopping! I was nearly catapulted over her head to land in a heap at Rachel's feet. Instead, I ended up sideways, only my left foot in a stirrup and hanging onto Molly's neck.

"That was some fancy riding buckaroo."

"Thanks. I come from a long line of Swedish cowboys."

Mostly I worked from five A.M. to eight at night with two meal breaks and some informal slack time. I watched with satisfaction my growing bank account and my increasing stash of shared tip money. After dinner, I often joined Ross, Mrs. M, Vincent and sometimes Uncle Pete on the porch of the employee housing. While Mrs. M fed me as much as I could eat, Vincent fed me books I would never have read otherwise: *A Sand County Almanac* by Aldo Leopold, *Profiles in Courage* by John F. Kennedy, and *Eichmann in Jerusalem: A Report on the Banality of Evil* by Hannah Arendt.

These were books that made me THINK in ways my high school classes had never done. Aldo Leopold wrote about taking care of the land one owns. Kennedy gave examples of people doing the right thing instead of the easy thing. Arendt's book was the most upsetting. Eichmann was a bureaucrat who helped run the Nazi machine that sent millions of Jews to death camps during World War Two. At his trial, he claimed he was not responsible; he was just following orders. I knew there was evil in the world, but I didn't realize that it could be thought of as banal, or ordinary.

On my ride north, I had met mostly wonderful people and seen nature at its best. Was the boy who assaulted the girl at the campground evil? He seemed to think there was not anything wrong with his behavior. Vincent told me that trying to understand the true nature of man was a lifetime job. Reading Arendt's book made me angry at Vincent for giving it to me. I was happy here in Alaska. I didn't want to think about evil in the world or children starving in Africa or South American dictators killing people. I wanted my summer to be about me. And Rachel. I decided not to pass on Arendt's book to her. And I stopped reading the lodge's copy of the Sunday New York Times. However, I started writing more in my journals; the one for my mother and my private one.

The next morning while I was cleaning Clarence, Ross stopped by to visit, carrying a fishing rod in a fancy case. "Your Uncle Pete doesn't often tell you that you are doing a good job —"

"Like never."

"Well, surprise, surprise. To recognize your hard work, he bought you a fishing license. Sunday evening you and I will be taking the drift boat out. Mrs. M will drive down river to pick us up."

"That sounds great."

"And wait, there's more. Instead of your 'Goodwill, start a conversation' fishing pole, you can have this quality L.L. Bean fly rod. We'll practice fly casting on land this evening."

"To keep?"

"Yes. A guest left it behind last summer. Had no luck and decided to give up fishing forever."

Just then Uncle Pete came out of the lodge. "Thanks, Uncle Pete," I called out.

"I just thought, that is, you are doing a good job, thought you should learn to fish," he said as he hurried by without stopping.

"I don't know why that man finds it so hard to give a compliment," Ross said.

"Unless you're a guest. Then —"

"He butters them up shamelessly."

"Rachel has Sunday evenings off. Can she come with us? She doesn't fish. She prefers to 'catch' her fish at the grocery store."

"The one you have been mooning over?"

"Not how I would put it, but yes."

"It will make less room for you for casting, so try not to hook her in the ear or something."

"Safety first. It's a deal."

Ross controlled the drift boat with expert use of the oars, backing the boat so I could fish an eddy, keeping the boat away from my line, and holding the boat steady in a current. He also talked with Rachel about her summer. I could tell she liked him. I was almost jealous. About halfway to our takeout point something big hit my line. I was so surprised I almost dropped the rod. That would have been bad. A huge fish broke the surface and leaped into the air. It looked silver in the sunlight as it twisted, trying to dislodge the hook.

"An Arctic grayling," Ross said. "A big one! Play him like we talked about."

The fish hit the water with a splash and made a run downstream. When the line tightened, I gave the rod a tug to set the hook. Game on. Ross coached me on when to let out line and when to reel in. It took some time. I stole a look at Rachel. She did not look excited. Finally, the grayling tired and I brought it to the side of the boat. Ross fished it out with a long-handled net. "Five pounds easy," Ross said with excitement.

Ross guided the boat to a sandbar. I struggled to take the hook out. I stood up holding the fish and Ross took a picture. Rachel refused to stand next to me. She looked angry. I realized I had never seen her look exactly like this.

"He's beautiful. Let him go. Out of water, he can't breathe."

I didn't know what to do. I didn't know what to say. She looked determined to have her way.

"I know, I know. Some of your clients fly thousands of miles and pay serious money to catch a fish like this. Please let him go."

"Catch and release," said Ross. He showed me how to hold the fish just under the water and sweep it back and forth to move water over its gills so it could take in oxygen. It felt okay to watch it swim away. When we reached the takeout point Mrs. M took a photo of Rachel and me. We both looked happy.

From that evening on, my relationship with Rachel shifted into a higher gear. In a way, it felt like shifting into a higher gear on my motorcycle and accelerating. On the trip north, I had joked that the bike and I were in a committed relationship. I would make it promises like "get us to Banff and I'll take you to a car wash." But what about Rachel and me?

For the rest of summer, I would sometimes go out after dinner on the river with Ross and a guest who had been skunked on that day's trip. We would take turns driving the sled boat and fishing. If the guest caught anything they were happy. There was usually whiskey drinking and cigar smoking. On one of these trips, I caught another Arctic grayling. Ross swore it was the same one I had caught before. It was delicious.

On one trip, a dense fog moved in while we were downstream. The fog deadened all sound including the putt-putt of the outboard motor. Ross kept to what he guessed was the middle of the channel. My job was to watch for our dock. On the edge of the river, I spotted a boulder that I had never seen before. Then the "boulder" stood up—ten feet of grizzly bear with fire in its eyes! But was it real? I heard the guest swearing, "That's a blankety-blank grizz!" Then it vanished. A few minutes later I spied our dock. We unloaded our gear and hauled it to the maintenance shed, aware that nearby in the fog was a thousand pounds of bear. The lodge had strict rules about food storage, garbage disposal and approaching wildlife but, when word got out there was a bear nearby, a few guests wanted to go into the woods to photograph it. Uncle Pete stopped them, then moved a lawn chair to the edge of lodge property and, armed with bear spray and a rifle, took up sentry duty.

Chapter Twelve

Getting to Know You

On our next Sunday off, Rachel and I took the motorcycle to Fairbanks. It felt good to be on the road again, away from work, Rachel's arms wrapped around me. We shopped and went to a movie, and I had prints made of ten of my photographs. After dropping Rachel off at her lodge, I sat out on the porch with Vincent. I showed him the prints.

"Jack, you have to learn to see the way the camera sees. All the time, look around. Even without a camera, make a U with your thumb and first finger and use that to frame possible photographs. We agreed that it is hard to photograph space. Your mountain photographs are okay but nothing special. You can break up the space, add depth by having a tree in the foreground. Or if there are shadows, puffy clouds, they will bring the mountains closer. It's tricky here in Alaska this time of year with the sun almost always above the horizon. Your shots of people are better. Having the instinct of when to 'pull the trigger' will work well for you."

"Your animal and bird pictures? They have personalities."

"I agree and it's what sells them."

"What's the secret?"

"Time and luck. Mostly time. For birds, I go where they are, and I sit down. And I watch. I try to make myself an unimportant, neutral entity. Can you understand that?"

"I think so," I answered. I told him about the old man at the café who had talked to me about sitting quietly in the woods. And I told him about my solitary night in the woods back home. Vincent listened carefully, but I sensed I wasn't telling him anything he didn't know.

"And luck?" I asked.

"One of my best-selling photos is the one of a Steller's Jay trying to decide if a bunch of grapes was food. There is something about his expression, the early morning sun and the way the end of the table cuts across at an angle that appeals to people. I have sold that picture over a hundred times. I snapped it on the way to an outhouse in a state park. Bears? I never get close enough to influence their behavior. I set up the telescopic lens—twelve hundred dollars well spent—and wait for them to do something. A stationary bear is a dull bear."

"Could I go out with you?"

"And give up time with Rachel? Honestly, no. Time in the woods? That is for me and the animals. If I brought another person, I would be bringing society with me, which would be counter to the point. Take your photographs and I'll critique them."

"Thanks. I appreciate that."

"One other thing. A lot of good photos are hidden in mediocre ones. Too much stuff, usually around the edges. This one. Put your thumbs on each side of the print so you have just a third of the scene. Better?"

"Much."

Then I asked him if he ever got lonely. As soon as I said it, I realized I had crossed a line. "I have the outdoors, travel, photography, my winter job. There isn't room for loneliness and there are times on a solitary hike when nature fills all my needs. Sometimes when I am walking, I have no desires except to be walking."

Me and horses, even mild-mannered Molly, did not really happen. After one of Rachel's older horses died during a ride, her boss bought a replacement that was not as well trained as advertised. Rachel took up the challenge. Sammy the horse did not like to be saddled and he seemed unconcerned that he would never be named Horse of the Month. He also didn't like to be roped so my job was to pretend I was a real cowboy by twirling a lasso over my head. Sammy would then give in and allow Rachel to saddle him.

Before training Sammy in the ring, Rachel would race him up and down the dirt road by the stables to tire him. I admired her courage. I took dozens of photographs of them racing by before I took one that was a winner. The sun behind the trees made shafts of sunlight and shadows. There was dust in the sunlight. Sammy had a slightly crazy look. Rachel was leaning forward with both a look of determination and joy. I want to spend the rest of my life taking pictures that good. Even Vincent approved of it.

On Sunday evenings, after playing a few games of volleyball, we got into the habit of walking down to the lake. I bet every guy at the court was jealous. One evening we turned off the main trail to follow a narrow, overgrown path and discovered a massive, concrete picnic table and benches on the edge of a cliff overlooking the lake. How or why such a monstrosity was there was a mystery. It became our special place. Away from both our jobs.

Even though it never became completely dark in the land of the midnight sun, bears were more active in the evenings. I carried a knife and perhaps I carried fantasies of being a hero as well. Rachel, being more rational, brought bear spray, a high-pressure can of mace that was meant to deter a charging bear. I wondered if it might just irritate them. The possibility of having a close encounter with the most fearsome predator in North America gave our meetings a certain edge.

"Did you take French or Spanish in high school?" Rachel asked.

"Well ... I ... two painful years of French."

"Painful in what way?"

"Painful for my teacher, Mrs. Grump. Not her real name, but appropriate."

"Let me guess. She didn't like the way you pronounced her beautiful language."

"Hated me for it. She grew up in France. Last term she stopped calling on me and gave me a C. Which was a big deal because my mother absolutely insisted that I get all A's and B's so going to college on scholarship would be an option. And except for that C in French and a C in Algebra II, that I deserved, I did it."

"Just two C's, I mean—"

"It didn't compute! Speaking was thirty percent of the grade and written work seventy percent. I got an A- in written work. It just didn't compute. I told my mother the teacher was an idiot and she slapped me for the first time ever. Not hard, maybe she tried to stop herself. She seemed horrified at what she had done. I grabbed my skateboard and went to the skate park. We never mentioned it after."

"My mother slapped me more than once. There is something terrible about it. Especially if you don't deserve it. My father used to spank me. My mother made him stop. Well, I guess we won't be speaking French this summer."

"Aren't there enough people speaking French, in France for example?"

"Wise guy. French and English. Translating. I had a French nanny when I was small. Can I read to you from this novel I'm translating?"

"*Oui, Mademoiselle.* Are there *parts de racee?*"

"Wise guy again. Not so far."

Rachel reading aloud then translating became part of our picnic table routine. Sometimes I would fall asleep. I loved the sound of her voice. Really, I loved everything about her.

On another night, she asked me to guess what she had wanted to be when she was fourteen. "A jockey?" I guessed.

"No."

"A veterinarian?"

"Like half the girls in my class? No."

"I give up."

"A crane operator. That sound I hear better not be a stifled laugh, mister. It was serious to me. I even had a picture of a crane on my bedroom wall."

"Okay."

"My parents had decided we should spend a weekend in New York, stay at the Ritz Carlton, and do some touristy things. They seemed desperate to come up with a way for us to spend time together. Our room was on the tenth floor. While my parents slept in that first morning, I stood at the window drinking an against-the-rules hotel room coffee and watching this giant crane, operated by an unseen hero, lift materials to the top of a new building. Just think. Way up there. Alone. In control. It sounded great to me. My parents had to force me to leave the room and go to Radio City Music Hall and the Empire State Building."

"You're making good money this summer, right? Doing well on tips?"

"Your point is?"

"Take your tip money and buy a motorcycle and the two of us could ride to New York together and you could show me the Empire State Building —"

"A good dream. Not going to happen. My parents would kill me if I didn't go back to college —"

"And ran off with a motorcycle man! But hey, let us dream about it. We could spend a whole day walking around the city looking for cranes. Take pictures of cranes. Climb up to visit the operator. Bring him, or her, a corned beef sandwich."

"Make fun if you want. My parents were smart enough to leave it alone. Speaking of which, they called last night. They want to fly out for a visit for a few days between my last day of work and flying home for college."

"You don't sound happy about it."

"I don't like traveling with them. My dad complains and my mom shops ... And there is something else, my friend Jack."

"Yes?"

"This is *our* Alaskan summer. I don't want to share it with anyone but you. I talked them out of it. I don't think they really wanted to visit, they just thought they should act interested."

"What have you told them about me?"

"Not much. What have you told your parents?"

"Not much. My mom is the one who calls. She really liked my high school girlfriend — boy, does that seem long ago."

"The secret lives of teenagers and the secret life of parents."

"I don't think my parents have any dark secrets. We do things together. I like being an only child. We talk. Our dinner table is kind of a free speech area. We have 'what if' conversations," I said.

"For example?"

"If there is life on other planets, would they like hamburgers? Or if we could read each other's minds, how long would it take for everyone to go crazy?"

"Sounds like fun. For some reason, we seldom have dinner together. My dad goes to, I don't know, Rotary meetings or whatever he sees as part of owning a car dealership. My mom is on committees. My older brother Ryan, who has flunked out of two colleges, never seems to be around."

"Sounds lonely."

"I guess. I was so glad to get away last summer and this summer. You're honest with each other?"

"I think so."

"Did you tell them about the time you snuck out to sleep alone in the woods?"

"At first I didn't tell anyone. I felt like it was between me and —"

"God?"

"Which is a subject that keeps coming up. I did. We were camped at ten thousand feet on the shoulder of Mt. Shasta the night before my mom and I climbed it. My dad had quit smoking, but his lungs were still shot so he stayed at base camp as our support team. We were enjoying the stars and it seemed a good time to share. They were okay about it."

"Tough climb?"

"Parts of it. We had to use ice axes and had to fasten crampons on our boots. Climbing that mountain was the hardest physical thing I had ever done. My mom took the lead. Every time she could sense I was flagging she would yell out, 'To the top!' And I would answer, 'To the top!'"

"But you and your mom stood on the summit together. That's beautiful. I cannot imagine my family climbing any mountain together. My dad's idea of exercise is driving a golf cart and my mother, who is a bit of a gym rat, would be worried about her make-up freezing or something."

"One of my best days ever."

"My mom and I did share a starry sky moment."

I slid down off the picnic table and sat beside Rachel. I put my arm around her. "Tell me," I said.

"I was twelve and we were on vacation at a dude ranch in New Mexico when my mom and I went on a midnight ride away from the lodge—"

"Singing cowgirl songs—"

"Don't interrupt. It was wonderful. It was an all-women ride. We soaked in a hot spring. The milky way was solid white. I remember feeling how ancient the world was."

"There is one thing I don't like about Alaska, the Land of the Midnight Sun. Just a few stars at the edge of the sky."

"We're star gazers without stars."

We started walking back to her lodge. At the same time, we raised our fists and yelled, "To the top!" We laughed. We kissed.

Chapter Thirteen

Friends

On the last night for each group of guests, there would be a "slide show" of their fishing adventures followed by a gathering around the fire pit. Ross would start the gathering with a few stories and his famous "in the air bowline knot." I saw it several times over the summer, and I still don't believe it. Ross would throw a piece of rope into the air and tie it into a bowline before catching it! It always blew the guests away. He enjoyed his moment in the spotlight. Vincent would follow with a bear story. The guests, of course, were expecting to hear about a near-death experience.

"I'm a little rusty so bear with me. The sourdoughs came to Alaska looking for gold-bearing streams. They had to bear heavy loads over Chilkoot Pass. It was a difficult climb, but they just had to grin and bear it. Some were barely alive when they reached the gold fields at Dawson. Some became lost and didn't know whether to bear right or bear left. There was little game on the barren plains. They just had to bear down and get the job done. Storms came in from the Bering Sea. Some struck it rich, and some made barely enough for a return ticket to Seattle. There were disputes. Calling a man a 'bare-faced liar' might lead to a gunfight. All the miners agreed with the right to bear arms. Bears were sometimes a problem, especially when mother bears came out of their dens after bearing one or two cubs. Hopefully, she had eaten enough berries in the fall ..."

By this point the guests would be groaning and calling out, "We can't bear it anymore" or "Please stop!" Mrs. M would start playing an old favorite on her guitar and the guests would join in singing. I loved it. It was like summer camp for adults. I asked Vincent about the rest of the bear story, but he said that was all there was. If it ever happened that guests didn't beg for mercy, Mrs. M would say "Enough, enough," and start singing.

On other evenings, Ross would work at leather craft, sitting at a picnic table in the shade of a tree by the dorm. Mrs. M would sit in a lawn chair and read. We had all adopted the Alaskan summer tradition of getting by on less sleep. I never got completely used to the midnight sun. About halfway through the summer, Ross asked me if I would like to replace my ugly, canvas, army surplus saddle bags with tooled leather ones. "Heck, yes."

Ross provided the leather at cost and the tools. I worked on the saddle bags while Ross fashioned wallets and belts and Mrs. M read. There was a shop back in Arizona that had no trouble selling everything Ross made. A few times, Rachel borrowed her lodge's pick-up and came over for a visit. We both agreed Ross and Mrs. M would have made perfect grandparents. When the saddlebags were done— they were easily the best thing I had ever made—Ross asked me if I wanted to learn to paddle a canoe on a fast-moving river. "Sure, why not?"

The lodge had two canoes, both beautiful, canvas Old Towns. Ross would paddle one canoe and I would paddle the other. We would work our way upstream then drift back down. Sometimes Ross would settle Mrs. M in the bow on lawn furniture cushions and call her his "Denali Queen." My challenge was to keep my canoe, against a strong and contrary current, exactly parallel to Ross's craft. Sometimes we seemed to be racing without quite admitting it. Ross taught me the "J" stroke: a way of keeping the canoe in a straight line without switching sides. He would often call out, "Strength, grace, and perfection, Jack, my man." I would think, *Easy for you to say, Old Man,* and try even harder.

"Jack," Mrs. M said to me one night, "I'm glad you and Rachel are having a good summer together."

"Me too. I wish summer would never end."

"Ross and I had some good summers when we were students at the University of Maine. He courted me by taking me on canoe or snowshoe outings. We were both on scholarship and could not afford to go out for dinner or to the movies even."

"Ancient history," Ross interjected.

"Sometimes Ross would sing to me."

I glanced at Ross. He was blushing.

"I majored in special education. Taught for twenty years around raising two boys. Both are now college professors. Ross got a degree in forestry and we moved to Colorado, but he never got along with management."

"Don't ask," Ross said to me.

"After the boys grew up, we discovered Alaska and your Uncle's Pete's Lodge. So here we are, on a twilight cruise in the twilight of our years."

"I am so happy to be here with you," I said, and boy, did I mean every word of it!

The next week, Rachel and I took the bike to a nearby lake for an evening swim. We swam back and forth in the narrow, shallow end of the lake. We raced. I won. We were about to get out when we heard a thrashing noise in the woods. A bear crashed out of the trees and dove into the lake, front legs outstretched, just like a human! We were thrilled until we realized the bear's trajectory, if he didn't change direction, put him on a collision course with us! The water was only three feet deep. We squatted down until just our heads were above water.

The bear was still swimming straight at us—or was it? It looked like it might be changing course. Rachel started to swim away. I grabbed her shoulder. We had been told that running, or in this case, swimming, would trigger the bear's pursuit instincts. Did the bear realize we were people? Could it smell us even though we were in up to our necks in water? The bear was approaching us faster than we could think! It seemed to look right at us. At the same time, we decided to take a breath and submerge. The bear missed us by less than ten feet. From underwater, it was just a dark shape moving past. We waited. We came to the surface just as the bear reached the far shore. I thought he looked back at us. He shook off like a dog and went into the woods.

Just after he disappeared, two teenage boys showed up on the other side of the lake.

"Did you see a bear?" one of the boys yelled.

"Why? Were you chasing one?" I yelled back.

"We heard something in the bushes over there," Rachel added, pointing away from the bear.

They charged off. I wondered what they thought they would do if they caught up with him.

"Idiots," Rachel called after them.

"That was definitely not a situation covered in our mandatory bear safety training," I said.

"I bet some of my fellow workers won't even believe me."

"Let's keep it to ourselves. Kind of like a souvenir of the summer," I suggested.

"Perfect," she agreed.

After we had changed and were on the motorcycle, Rachel asked me, "If the bear had come right at us, would you, I don't know, have whacked it on the nose or something?"

"Of course."

"You are a fool for love."

One evening Rachel and I went to a sled dog demonstration. The "sled" was a quad with the engine removed. If you are a Husky, running is what you do. They can run for hours without tiring. For them, it isn't work, it's joy. The dogs not chosen for the demonstration howled in protest at the end of their chains. The six-dog team pulled the musher around an obstacle course at a remarkable speed. This relationship between man and animal I could understand more than the one between man and horse. I imagined what it would be like to be on a midnight run in winter under the northern lights. Rachel would be on the sled wrapped in blankets, only her beautiful face showing as we raced across the Arctic landscape.

Chapter Fourteen

Denali at Last

That Saturday, I received some great news. Rachel had the next day off and Ross offered to do my airport run so I could have a full day off as well. Denali National Park! We had been into the park on the motorcycle, but private vehicles were only allowed as far as the Eielson Visitor Center. We signed up for the guided bus tour that went all the way to Wonder Lake at the base of Denali. We were on the first bus out.

Immensity! The landscape and a feeling. Both hard to describe. Not a friendly-looking environment, even during the summer. Much of the terrain was without trees. The Nenana River twisted back and forth across a wide valley. Man's presence at the entrance and this one road hardly seemed to matter. Here was an eco-system of six million acres mostly unchanged since the end of the last ice age.

The vast valley is home to black bears, grizzly bears, Dall sheep, caribou, elk, moose, wolves, coyotes, and numerous smaller species. To Rachel and me, the feeling that people don't belong here was a good feeling. People have overrun so much of the world, it was good to be in a place protected by law, size, and the harsh climate. The driver-guide did a good job of sharing information about the park, and she gave us a warning. "You know you are in the wilderness when you are not at the top of the food chain. If you encounter wildlife, how that encounter goes is up to the wildlife. Fortunately, none of the animals see us as food … most of the time." I wondered if I would dare sleep out alone in Denali Park. If I did, would I lie awake listening for bears?

"I feel like we have been dropped onto another planet," Rachel said.

"I was thinking the same thing," I said.

As we traveled toward the lake, the sparse forest gave way to alpine tundra. No trees, but millions of wildflowers. The bus reached the end of the pavement and continued on a narrow gravel road just barely wide enough for two buses to pass each other. Denali lay hidden in the clouds ahead—until it wasn't. "The mountain is out!" came the cry from many throats. We poured off the bus, some people bumping and shoving. I had seen the top third several times while on the river, but now, from this distance, seeing the whole mountain was something special. Denali: 20,310 feet, highest peak in North America, part of my Alaskan dream.

I took a dozen photographs even though I knew there would be nothing special about them, artistically speaking. We walked down the road, away from the frenzied photographers. With our arms around each other, we just looked at the mountain; the most impressive natural wonder either of us had ever seen. Low clouds moved in, obscuring the bottom half of the mountain.

The guide herded us back on the bus. We still had many miles of gravel road to go before reaching Wonder Lake. Rachel fell asleep with her head on my shoulder. Sometime later, the guide stopped the bus. She looked through her binoculars at a brown shape a long way off. Grizzly? I took out my newly purchased field glasses. Yes, on a kill, being harassed by four wolves. Ravens hovered, hoping for a snack. The wolves took turns dashing in, then stopping just out of reach of the bear's swiping claws while another member of the pack grabbed a morsel. I whispered one word into Rachel's ear. She came fully awake in an instant.

The guide allowed us to get off the bus. She set up a powerful telescope and we took turns. "Looks like an elk has joined the cycle of life and death in the park," she said. The bear stopped trying to feed and concentrated on attacking the wolves. Eventually, the wolves moved on, looking for an easier meal. "They'll be back after the bear has eaten his fill."

Our next unscheduled stop was for a small herd of Dall sheep on a near-vertical cliff near the road. The males stand three feet tall at the shoulder and weigh about two hundred pounds. They have large, curved horns. The females are smaller with lighter, straighter horns. They are both pure white. In the summer they protect themselves from predators by staying on steep terrain. In winter they move to lower elevations where their white coats help camouflage them. The males are known for their violent head butting when they compete for the favor of a female. Like their cousins, the big horn sheep in Banff, this group thrilled us with their ability to climb and leap surefootedly from rock to rock.

A few minutes later we braked for a herd of caribou crossing the road. They were close enough that we could hear the clicking sound their ankles make when they walk. It's made by a tendon slipping back and forth over their heel bone. Caribou and reindeer are of the same species. They rely on speed to escape predators. Their top speed is forty-eight miles an hour! Predators take down the sick or older animals which helps preserve the health of the herd.

Eighty-five miles from the park entrance we arrived at Wonder Lake. We had a half hour to eat a lunch packed for us by Mrs. M. When the mountain is out, it's reflected in Wonder Lake. Even though this scene has been photographed thousands of times, I think everybody on the bus hoped the thin clouds veiling the mountain would sail away. After lunch Rachel and I waded into the lake, slipping on the round rocks and holding on to each other. Wonder Lake is fed by the glaciers on Denali. Boy was it cold. Still, it felt good to wash the road dust off our faces and arms. A shout went up for the second time that day, "The mountain is out!"

I stumbled back to shore for my camera but asked Rachel to stay where she was. I squatted down and got a shot of the mountain with the lake and Rachel in the foreground washing her face. I knew that this was one of my better photographs of the whole summer. A few minutes later, the clouds moved back in.

We traveled seven more miles to the historic mining town of Kantishna. Over a hundred years ago the town had been the center of extensive gold and silver mining efforts. We visited the cabin of a rough pioneer woman named Fannie Quigley. She was known as a hard-drinking, foul-mouthed hunter and trapper and a favorite cook working out of tent kitchens to feed the miners. She wintered over for decades, survived two husbands, and died in 1944, age seventy-four.

On the return trip, the atmosphere on the bus was hot and sleepy. But Denali had one more surprise for us. On the shore of a lake near the road, a mother grizz and cub were foraging for edible plants. Much of a bear's diet is vegetarian. The bears were about two hundred yards away. Our guide reminded us that a grizzly can run a hundred yards in six seconds! She told us to stay within the outline of the bus if we decided to get off and to get back on immediately if told to do so. The bears ignored us. Using my telephoto lens, I tried to capture their personalities. I don't think I succeeded.

The rest of the trip back to the park entrance was uneventful.

Usually when Rachel rode on the back of my motorcycle, I could feel she was tense. After all, she wasn't on a horse and she wasn't in charge. On the way home from our day in the park, I could tell she was relaxed, trusting. Instead of looking over my shoulder, she rode with the side of her head between my shoulder blades. "Don't fall asleep," I cautioned.

Chapter Fifteen

Endless Summer-Not!

During one of our twilight paddles, Ross pointed out a great fishing spot on the far side of the river from the lodge and a mile upstream. There was a strong current that made it difficult for a solo canoeist to angle across successfully. Ross challenged me to paddle across, beach the canoe, and catch a few small trout for breakfast. I practiced off and on during the summer. Gradually my stroke got almost strong enough to overcome the current. Mastering this skill was important to me. I wanted to impress Ross and I wanted to teach myself perseverance.

Finally, the day after visiting Denali, I made it. The canoe sliced through the water like an arrow. I beached the canoe and caught two pan-sized trout. I returned to the lodge and knocked on Ross's door. "I did it. Here you go. I caught them. You clean them for our breakfast tomorrow."

"Good man. If you come back next summer, I'll teach you to row the drift boat."

"It's a deal." I felt proud to shake his hand.

I must have been busy working and it snuck up on me—only a week left of summer. Rachel was leaving the day after Labor Day. I was leaving a week later. Last Sunday she'd had to cover for a wrangler who left early. After my morning airport run, I was busy helping Uncle Pete do year-end maintenance on the sled boats. I hadn't seen much of Uncle Pete all summer except when he was giving me my marching orders. Besides guiding, he was busy eating, drinking, playing cards with the guests, making the metal stake ring at horseshoes, and, if rumors were correct, making "mystery runs" into Fairbanks to visit a girlfriend.

As far as guests went, part of my job as all-around helper was to be seen and not heard except for brief, polite conversations. On the other hand, Ross, Mrs. M and Vincent helped make my summer. Three remarkable and interesting people. Other than neighbors back home, they were my first adult friends. From them, I learned far more than leather craft, canoeing, photography, and making sandwiches. I learned that it was possible to follow one's own path; to be the person you want to be.

And then there was Rachel and a final rendezvous at our picnic table. Even though it seemed unlikely we would ever see each other again, I knew that I would never forget her. Perhaps, God willing, we would both be back next year. Not yet September and there was already a chill in the air. It now got dark before midnight. The stars were out again. We wore sweaters and brought a blanket with us. We sat side by side, wrapped in the blanket, our backs against the table, facing the lake.

"I brought coffee and left-over scones from the dining room," Rachel said, rummaging in her day pack, "and some expensive cheese." She knew me. I was always hungry.

"Delicious. One of those moments I wish could last forever," I said, feeling sorry for myself.

"Lots of good conversations, good times. Swimming with the bear."

"My first horseback ride. I don't think Molly ever liked me after that."

"Denali Park. Wild animals. The mountain. Ross and Mrs. M, Vincent."

"Beyond awesome."

"The ride home from the park on your motorcycle."

"Yes?"

"With my arms around you, trusting you, not looking over your shoulder—that was one of the happiest times of my life!"

"I am so glad. I could feel it."

"And now the world is out there waiting for us."

"For you, university and French. I now see learning a new language is a way to see the world differently. I liked listening to you read out loud."

"For you, skiing, adventures, maybe photos in National Geographic, climbing Denali!"

"Maybe. Completely different world than Mt. Shasta: white outs, extreme temperatures, high winds, weather delays, stuck in a tent with a climbing partner for days. That would be okay if the climbing partner was *vous*."

"Seems unlikely. I'm dreaming more of a long horseback wilderness ride."

"Dreams ..."

"Wouldn't it be great if I visited you and we climbed Shasta together?"

"All you have to do is buy a ticket, get on a plane to San Francisco. I'll be the one waiting for you with a great big grin on my face."

"Do you think your parents would like me?"

"Are you kidding? Instant love fest."

"This summer has been better than ..."

"College?"

"Yes. Better than high school?"

"Yes. All that being inside. And I still have the journey back home."

There was a short silence. I was thinking about Mt. Shasta City and my parents. I assumed Rachel was also thinking of her hometown.

"More cheese?" she asked me, breaking the silence.

"Thanks. You are thinking really hard. I can tell."

"I was thinking that here, under more stars than earlier in the summer, a summer of new experiences, we could leave some things from our past behind," said Rachel.

"Then hug a tree?"

"Don't be a wise guy. And don't give me that confused look."

"Okay, okay," I said, finishing the last of my coffee.

"I leave behind my dream of being a crane operator."

"I give up trying to like horses."

"I will never have a bowling average over two hundred."

"You take it seriously? Something I didn't know about you. I will never be a movie star."

"You didn't really dream of—you don't think you could play the solitary adventurer?"

"No. Vincent could play that role."

"Yes, an interesting man."

"Are we giving up old dreams to make room for new ones?" I asked, with that odd sensation of my heart being in my throat.

"In an uncertain world, all I can say is, maybe."

"My turn," Rachel said, breaking away. "I will never really like my mom. Oh, I feel bad saying that. We are just so completely different."

"Ouch … I will never make the Olympic Ski Team. Future time. Is there something you never want to be?"

"Bitter."

"I can't—"

"Like my older brother. And angry. Doesn't say much, but I can … smell it. I'll always love my parents, but I'll never live in my hometown."

"Until this summer I never thought I would live anywhere else. And I never want to be homeless," I said.

"That seems unlikely."

"There were a few homeless men who hung out at our skateboard park. They used to have jobs, families, but something went wrong. One of them froze to death last winter."

"That sounds lonely. Death. What the heck is that about?"

I told her about the fatal accident. I told her about holding the dying man in my arms. I just let loose. Said whatever came into my mind. I think I came close to ruining our evening but I just could not help myself.

"Did he know he was dying? Did he know you were there?"

"I think so. It didn't seem spiritual but maybe I was too in shock to sense his soul ... leaving. It just seemed really, really sad."

"That was a good thing you did, Jack, my man. Wow. We are supposed to be celebrating. I even brought coffee and scones ... I'm going to miss our time here at our very own picnic table."

"If it was wood, we could carve our initials," I said.

"And come back twenty years later?"

"Why not?" I said.

"A toast to the future," Rachel said, taking a sip of her coffee and handing the cup to me. "Let's pretend that the universe can hear us tonight."

"Us? Two little specks of nothing?"

"Yes. A thousand times, yes. We are as important as any other two specks," said Rachel, her voice almost rising to a shout.

"You want me to talk to the stars?"

"Yes. To celebrate being here on good, old planet earth under the stars, millions of years old. I know you understand. I'll go first."

Rachel climbed up on the picnic table. She leaned back and gave a wolf howl that echoed lightly across the lake.

"I don't know why I did that."

"It was beautiful. You're beautiful."

"Let me go again. Ask something ... Help me let go of my miseries!" in a voice that might have carried all the way back to her lodge. She took a few steps and jumped off the table. She said, "That felt so good." I had a momentary feeling that I didn't know her as well as I thought I did. I climbed on the picnic table without the slightest idea what I was going to say. How often does one call out to the stars?

"Inhale, exhale, inhale and speak," Rachel said.

I felt annoyed with her. I was getting there on my own. "I am so unfinished."

"Louder, so the universe can hear you."

"I AM SO UNFINISHED!"

That night I lay on my narrow bed, in my narrow room with its narrow window and I thought about the wide-open possibilities of life.

Chapter Sixteen

Trial by Fire

On the Sunday morning before Labor Day, Mrs. M got up at four in the morning as usual. Walking to the lodge she sensed something was wrong. SMOKE! She got on the short-wave radio. The fire was on our side of the river five miles south of us. The winds were calm but expected to rise in the afternoon. A fire crew would be arriving to use the lodge as a base. She pounded on Uncle Pete's door. He was a heavy sleeper, but it woke the rest of us up.

Vincent and Ross came out of their rooms. "Is that smoke I smell?" Vincent asked.

As Mrs. M kept pounding on Uncle Pete's door, she filled us in on what was happening, including a radio notice to prepare for evacuation. Uncle Pete came to the door looking annoyed and as if he had had a tough night. He took one breath and said the word "smoke" along with an impressive string of cuss words.

Uncle Pete took charge. He assigned Ross and me the job of beaching our three boats on the far side of the river using a canoe as a shuttle. Mrs. M gathered up important papers. Uncle Pete woke up the guests and ordered them to pack. Mrs. M would drive them to the airport and wait to meet the incoming guests and explain the situation. Ross would use a sled boat to patrol the river in case anyone needed to be evacuated. Vincent and Uncle Pete were members of the volunteer fire brigade and I had been through their basic training. We would join the fire crew when they arrived.

I got back from moving the boats just as Mrs. M was about to leave with the guests. She ran over and gave me a hug. "Don't be a hero, Jack. Stick close to Uncle Pete." If I wasn't afraid before, I was then. While we waited for the fire crew to arrive, we changed into our fire-resistant clothing and raided the kitchen for a quick breakfast of sandwiches and coffee.

Smoke arrived in slow-moving swirls from the south. Vincent got out a ladder and climbed on the roof of the dorm with binoculars. "I can see a huge plume of smoke; can't tell which way the fire is moving." Right then, I sensed we were all worried that we might lose the lodge. And I realized I might lose my bike. The river. Maybe it was a crazy idea, but maybe not. The rocky bottom was slippery. I managed to ride the bike into the river until the water was at the bottom of the crankcase.

I wedged the kickstand between two rocks, put my camera in the saddle bags, waded back to shore and put my boots back on just as the fire crew arrived. We were issued helmets, Pulaskis—a combination digging and chopping tool— and "shake and bakes." "Shake and bakes" are emergency metallic shelters that can be used if you are overtaken by the fire. They were designed to protect you from the heat and to provide some breathable oxygen. Our goal was to create a fire break about two miles from the lodge by clearing an area of vegetation down to bare dirt. We hiked to our assigned area double time.

I could tell Uncle Pete was suffering but he didn't complain. "Jack, it's like we're in the army. We do whatever the crew boss tells us."

"Yes, Sir," I answered.

As we neared our area, the smoke was thicker and seemed to be flowing directly toward the lodge. I believed the work I was to do that day might be the most important of my life. I dug and chopped, dug and chopped until I felt like my arms might fall off. The smoke got thicker and thicker. It carried a suggestion of heat. We kept working. Time was measured by how much ground cover we reduced to bare dirt. To take a quick break and drink water from a canteen was heaven. I used up my reserves, but it didn't matter. Everyone else was still working. I felt like I had been working for days. The lodge and my family and Rachel barely existed. All there seemed to be was smoke and swinging the Pulaski. Then it changed. There seemed to be more heat in the smoke and the smoke was moving faster. When there were breaks, we could see the smoke glowing orange as the fire crested the ridge about a half mile away. It slowed as it worked its way downhill. The crew boss called for a ten-minute water break. "We should be able to stop it."

Just as the fire reached the bottom of the canyon below us, the wind seemed to change. "An up-canyon wind," Uncle Pete muttered, looking worried. When bigger pines ignited, they sent flames shooting into the sky, but mostly the fire kept near the ground, moving steadily, making crackling sounds, and moaning. Something changed. I wasn't sure what, but the hair stood up on my forearms. Briefly, I remembered playing firefighters with my friends in the woods behind our house. This was as far from play acting as one could get.

"The fire is making its own wind," Uncle Pete muttered as he looked down the line for a sign from the crew boss. Too late! All the other sounds of the fire were wiped out by a roar like an oncoming freight train.

"DEPLOY! DEPLOY!" The word was passed down the line.

"Deploy" meant we were no longer fighting the fire. It meant the fire was hunting us! We had no place to hide, no time to run. "Deploy" meant you climbed inside your "shake and bake" and prayed that you would survive. Inside the tube you would hold your breath as long as possible, ignoring the tremendous build-up of heat.

"Deploy" meant you were about to spend time in hell!

I froze for a moment when I heard the call to deploy come out of the smoke. My uncle grabbed my shoulder and shook me. We pulled the shelters out of our packs. Uncle Pete pushed me toward a large rock and helped me into the shelter. We were already being blasted by intense heat pushed along in front of the firestorm. Uncle Pete got into his own shelter and rolled against me. Partly protected by the large rock and my uncle's body increased my chances of survival.

Oxygen. The most precious commodity in the world.

The noise and heat beat down on me like a physical force. Even through the shelter, I felt like I was being pressed down into the earth. Moment by moment I could feel the forces against me getting stronger. How strong was my will to survive? I fought the irrational desire to climb out of the shelter and make a run for it.

Despite my fire-resistant clothing, I felt that my skin might catch on fire. My whole body was getting hotter and hotter. I was afraid to breathe but I had to take a few shallow breaths to keep from passing out. I tried to slow down my whole body so it would need less oxygen. I railed against the fire by saying—no, thinking; saying would use too much energy—*I'm too young to die.*

Finally, I entered a place of disbelief.

A small part of my brain, in order to keep me from giving up, decided that what was happening wasn't real. I tried to let a vision of swimming in Wallowa Lake take over my brain. It partly worked. My feelings of panic subsided. With all my being I pretended I could feel the cold water and breathe the smoke-free air. Soon, however, this delusion was broken by Uncle Pete squirming against me. I prayed he would survive.

Time.

My desperate daydream of swimming faded and time slowed until the only way to measure it was that it was getting hotter. At what seemed to me a point near death, a miracle happened. The heat, the wind, the noise that had crushed me inside the shelter, all seemed to flow away. I peeked out. The smoke was still thick, but the heat seemed to be moving away with the flames that had passed over us and were now headed for the lodge!

My uncle groaned and rolled away from me. We both crawled out of our shelters but were unable to stand. On our hands and knees, we carefully inhaled and exhaled. Uncle Pete looked as if he might pass out. I managed to croak, "Are you all right?"

"No. I think my lungs are burned. Help me stand up."

I got up. I felt dizzy. I also felt great joy in surviving. I wondered if everyone else had survived. I helped Uncle Pete stand up. I held him while he took careful, shallow breaths.

"My shirt feels like it's on fire. Help me get it off," he said.

His back looked like it had a severe sunburn. I emptied my water bottle on him. The crew boss, Vincent, and the rest of the crew appeared.

"Boy, am I glad to see you two. You had the worst of it. We all survived," said Vincent. "Pete, you're not looking good."

"My lungs are burned. Can't get enough oxygen," Uncle Pete rasped.

"Vincent," I said. "We have to do something. He saved my life."

"It's two miles to the lodge, but there's a clearing about halfway with an overgrown logging road that starts near the lodge. If we could get him there … I'll run to the lodge, get the old pickup, grab a chainsaw and bushwhack my way back."

"I'll help carry him," I said.

The crew boss put his hand on my shoulder and said, "Every man reaches his limit. I can see you've reached yours. I'll have the Swedes do it."

Two large men stepped forward and lifted Uncle Pete in the two-man fireman's carry and set off. I followed along behind. Vincent left running. When we reached the clearing, we could hear the sweet sound of a pick-up with a faulty muffler approaching. Vincent burst through the brush. I helped Uncle Pete into the cab and sat beside him. He was looking gray, unfocused. Vincent told him that the fire had missed the lodge, but Uncle Pete didn't respond. I put my arm around him to keep him from falling forward. Vincent and a crew member cut down some small trees so there would be room to turn around. Once we were pointed in the right direction all the firefighters climbed on board. Standing up, they held onto the truck and each other.

When we got to the lodge and Uncle Pete saw it was unscathed, he said, "It's a miracle."

Just then Ross pulled up to the dock and rushed over. "Boy, am I glad to see your ugly mug," he said.

"Did Mrs. M make it to the airport?" Uncle Pete asked.

"Yes, she's fine. I made two trips downriver. Evacuated twenty campers, left them at Rachel's lodge."

The crew boss came over. "The highway is still open. Transport will be here in thirty-forty minutes."

"Pete, I'm taking you to the clinic," Vincent said.

"I'm going with you," I said.

"No," said Uncle Pete. "I have a job for you. You have some thirsty and hungry firefighters on your hands. Open up the kitchen, raid the refrigerator."

"Yes, Sir. And thanks for saving my life."

"You are welcome. Just promise to make good use of it."

The crew cleaned up at the outside faucet. After I set out sandwich makings, juice, iced tea and turned on the coffee maker, I called Rachel.

"I absolutely need to see you right now!" she yelled into the phone.

I waded into the river with my boots on and started up the motorcycle. The back wheel spun on the wet rocks, but I managed to avoid falling and bounced up the beach to the road. At the Broken K Ranch Rachel was in the parking lot, waiting for me with open arms. After a long embrace, I told her about surviving the firestorm. I got the shakes. She cried.

"This is it, isn't it? We have twenty extra guests and I'm leaving in the morning. The end of our best summer ever."

As I drove away, Rachel must have remembered what I had said about my mother hating tattoos, because she called out, "Don't get a tattoo!"

My vision was a little bleary the first few miles going back to my lodge.

Chapter Seventeen

Aftermath

When I returned to the lodge, Mrs. M and our last guests of the season were there. I helped with dinner. There was still smoke in the air and the atmosphere in the dining room was subdued. Vincent arrived and reported that Uncle Pete had been transferred to the hospital in Fairbanks and would be out of service for four or five days. After dinner, Vincent took me aside. "You'll need to drive the other sled boat. You've had enough practice. Just follow me. When I stop at an eddy, you wait, go next. I'll explain to the guests that you won't be talking fishing lore, but after dinner, I'll put on a photo show where I talk about the river and wildlife."

So now, in addition to being a handyman and chauffeur, I was a river guide. Plus, I had extra work to do helping Mrs. M get the lodge ready to be closed down. When Uncle Pete returned after three days, he helped where he could but was still weak.

The season ended. I drove the guests to the airport. The next day I drove Vincent, Mrs. M, Ross, and Uncle Pete to the airport. When I got back to the lodge, the winter caretaker and his wife had set up their trailer. Boy, did I feel sad about leaving. I rode north to Fairbanks where I had made an appointment at a cycle shop for an oil change and a lube job. While I waited, I looked at the twenty photographs I had developed out of the hundreds I had taken. My favorite was the one of Rachel washing her face in Wonder Lake with Denali in the background.

The mechanic brought out the bike, cleaned up and ready to go. I settled myself on my trusty steed. I was excited about being on the road again: helping Daryl with his cabin for a few days, taking the ferry part way home, seeing the Alaskan coast, whale watching, and the final ride home from Seattle on the interstate. I imagined myself cresting Siskiyou Pass on the Oregon border and seeing Mt. Shasta, my home mountain, again. I had had the adventure of a lifetime and I had the photos and the journal to prove it.

As I pulled out of the parking lot, the mechanic called out, "Good luck with the fishing."

Epilogue

After my great Alaska adventure, I worked with my friend, Davie, on bridge construction, saved my money, and enrolled in college. I spent the next four summers at my uncle's lodge as a fishing guide. After graduating with a teaching degree from the University of California, Davis, I returned to my old high school to teach history and English and coach the school's ski team. Rachel and I kept in touch for a while until she moved permanently to France. The next summer I spent six weeks hiking in the Swiss Alps.

And someday I hope to meet an adventurous young lady who will be ...

About the Author

Warren Carlson began his adventurous life when, at age fourteen, he slept alone in the woods for the first time and discovered that the world was a friendly and beautiful place. Other adventures followed: climbing Mt. Shasta three times and Mt. Ranier once; solitary hikes in several national parks; alpine excursions in France, Switzerland, Spain, and Azerbaijan; Peace Corps Volunteer in the middle east; travel to India, Kashmir, Turkey, Ireland, England and yes, a solitary motorcycle ride to Alaska where he met some of the characters depicted in this book while others have been made up or transferred from other adventures.

Carlson describes himself as a job vagabond. His employment adventures include ski instructor, actor-director-playwright, special needs teacher, newspaper reporter, carpenter, cowboy, ski area management, house designer and builder, and tour guide in three national parks.

His literary credits include numerous short stories and poetry. (*Northern Journeys, Spectrum, Jefferson Journal* and others.) His plays have been produced in several venues including Spokane Repertory, Spokane, Washington; Actors' Theatre, Ashland, Oregon; and the Metta Theatre, Taos, New Mexico. He holds a B.A. in Creative Writing from the University of California, Santa Barbara.

"I've written the book that I would have loved to read when I was fifteen."

WarrenCarlsonWriter.com   FathomPublishing.com